ArtScroll Youth Series

Rabbi Nosson Scherman / Rabbi Meir Zlotowitz

General Editors

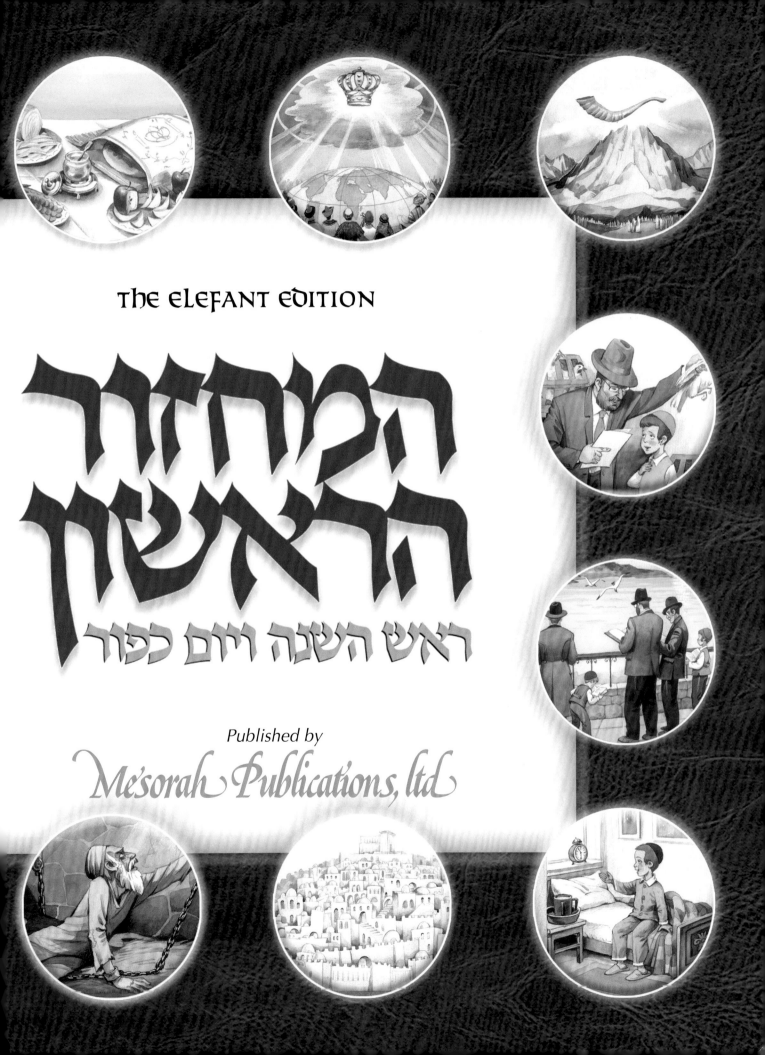

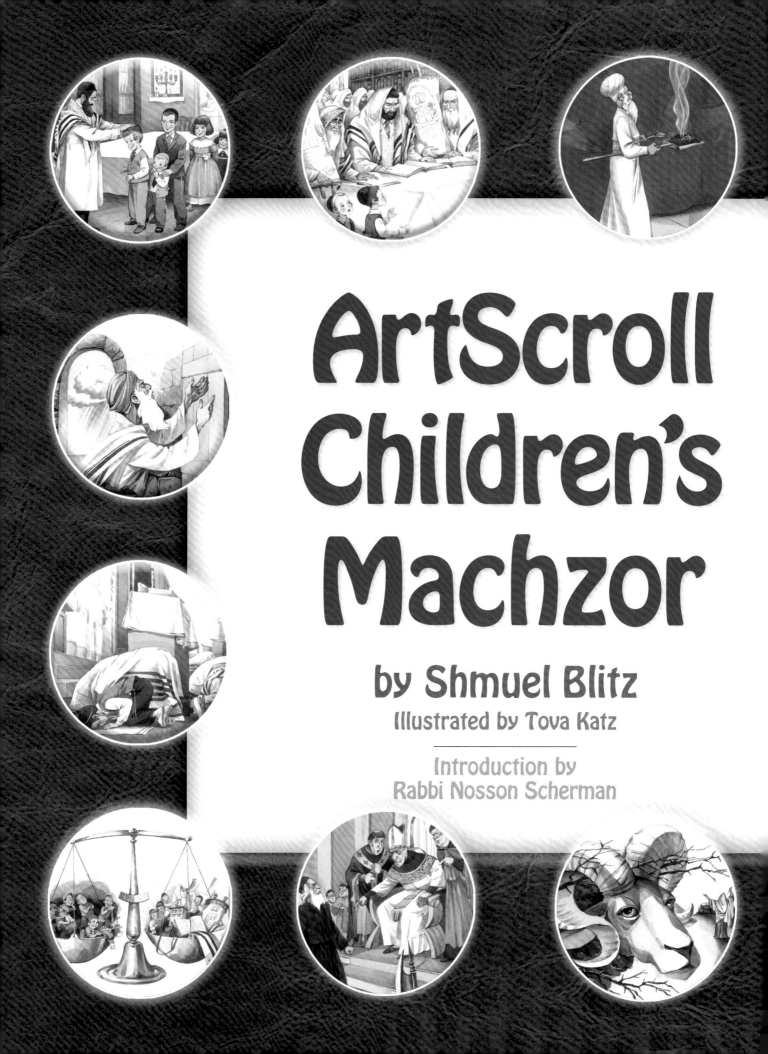

ArtScroll
Children's
Machzor

by Shmuel Blitz

Illustrated by Tova Katz

Introduction by
Rabbi Nosson Scherman

We dedicate this Machzor
in loving memory of our parents

ר׳ אברהם ניסן בן ר׳ אהרן גדול הכהן ז״ל Grushko

ר׳ שלמה יצחק בן ר׳ חיים יוסף מאיר ז״ל Elefant

פעסיל גיטל בת ר׳ ישעי׳ יצחק הכהן ע״ה Elefant

ר׳ יוסף בן ר׳ שמעון ז״ל Hirsch

Leah and Mendy Elefant and Family
Faigy and Berish Elefant and Family

And in loving memory of our father and brother

ר׳ יעקב בן שמואל ז״ל Raps

ר׳ שמואל בן יעקב ז״ל Raps

Leah and Effy Raps and Family

They raised families loyal to Torah and mitzvos,
and dedicated to the eternity of Klal Yisrael.

It is fitting that their memory is honored by this Machzor
that will bring the joy of Judaism to young children
and inspire them to follow in the footsteps of previous generations.

FIRST EDITION *First Impression … August 2009 / Second Impression … August 2011*
ARTSCROLL SERIES® / **ARTSCROLL CHILDREN'S MACHZOR FOR ROSH HASHANAH / YOM KIPPUR — THE ELEFANT EDITION**
© Copyright 2009, by MESORAH PUBLICATIONS, Ltd., 4401 Second Avenue / Brooklyn, NY 11232 / (718) 921-9000 / www.artscroll.com

ISBN 10: 1-4226-0910-3 / ISBN 13: 978-1-4226-0910-1
Typography by CompuScribe at ArtScroll Studios, Ltd.
Printed in the United States of America • Bound by Sefercraft, Quality Bookbinders, Ltd., Brooklyn N.Y. 11232

Table of Contents

Rosh Hashanah — ראש הַשָּׁנָה

Yom Kippur — יוֹם כִּיפּוּר

Introduction
Coming Back to Hashem

Once there were two children. Each one wanted to make things with tools, so their parents bought them hammers, nails, and pieces of wood. The parents said, "We are glad that you want to make things. It's up to you to decide what you will make. When you are finished, please show us."

One of them decided he wanted to make shelves for books and toys. His parents heard the sound of the hammer banging nails into wood and waited to see what he would bring them. When he was finished, he called them and said, "Look what I made! It's a bookcase!"

His parents hugged and kissed him. It was not as nice as a bookcase they could buy in a store, but they carried it to his room and helped him fill the shelves. They were proud of him.

The other child took the hammer and began banging nails into the furniture and even into the windows! The parents heard sounds they did not like. They ran in and saw what he was doing. They were not happy. They took away the hammer and nails and wanted to punish him.

He cried and cried. He said he was sorry and would not do it again. But the windows were still broken and the furniture was ruined. His parents could not trust him with tools anymore.

We are all like the second child. Hashem gives us a *neshamah*. He wants us to do mitzvos and not do *aveiros* — but He lets us decide what we will do. Many times we don't listen to what the Torah says. What should Hashem do to us? Our parents take away the hammer if we use it to break things, even if we say we are sorry. Should Hashem take away our *neshamah*? Should He say that we are like children who ruin the furniture and break windows and we can't fix them just by saying we are sorry?

Hashem does not do that. He says that if we are really sorry, we can do *teshuvah*. *Teshuvah* means that we start doing what the Torah says and stop doing *aveiros*. Hashem loves us and wants us to do *teshuvah*. He says that If we really mean it, He will erase all the *aveiros*, and it will be as if we never did anything wrong.

Rosh Hashanah is the day when we say to Hashem, "We want to do *teshuvah* and try to become perfect — just the way You wanted us to be." And Yom Kippur is the day when Hashem says, "I see that you really want to be good, and I forgive you."

This *Machzor* for very young children has many of the things that we do on Rosh Hashanah and Yom Kippur, and it has many of the *tefillos* that we daven. We hope that it will help Hashem's beloved children understand what these days mean to our parents and to us. Hashem wants us to do *teshuvah* and He wants to forgive us.

When we get older, we will have the big *Machzor*, and daven like our parents. Meanwhile, let's use this *Machzor*. It's just for us. Let's daven that we, our families, and all of Klal Yisrael will have a good and healthy year and that *Mashiach* will come soon.

Elul 5769 / August 2009   **Rabbi Nosson Scherman**

The author dedicates his work to his granddaughter,

Ariel Blitz

הַדְלָקַת נֵרוֹת רֹאשׁ הַשָּׁנָה / Rosh Hashanah Candle Lighting

On each night of Rosh Hashanah, the following blessing is said.

Blessed are You, Hashem, our God, King of the universe, Who has made us holy with His mitzvos, and commanded us to light the Yom Tov candle.

בָּרוּךְ אַתָּה יהוה אֱלֹהֵינוּ מֶלֶךְ הָעוֹלָם, אֲשֶׁר קִדְּשָׁנוּ בְּמִצְוֹתָיו, וְצִוָּנוּ לְהַדְלִיק נֵר שֶׁל יוֹם טוֹב.

When Rosh Hashanah comes out on Shabbos, we say this blessing instead.

Blessed are You, Hashem, our God, King of the universe, Who has made us holy with His mitzvos, and commanded us to light the Shabbos candle and the Yom Tov candle.

בָּרוּךְ אַתָּה יהוה אֱלֹהֵינוּ מֶלֶךְ הָעוֹלָם, אֲשֶׁר קִדְּשָׁנוּ בְּמִצְוֹתָיו, וְצִוָּנוּ לְהַדְלִיק נֵר שֶׁל שַׁבָּת וְשֶׁל יוֹם טוֹב.

On each night of Rosh Hashanah, we add the following blessing.

Blessed are You, Hashem, our God, King of the universe, for keeping us alive, taking care of us, and bringing us to this time.

בָּרוּךְ אַתָּה יהוה אֱלֹהֵינוּ מֶלֶךְ הָעוֹלָם, שֶׁהֶחֱיָנוּ וְקִיְּמָנוּ וְהִגִּיעָנוּ לַזְּמַן הַזֶּה.

Did You Know??
From the time they are married, women light two candles to honor Shabbos and Yom Tov. In many families, the custom is to add one more candle after each new child is born. And so they light two candles plus one more for each child. Some communities have different customs.

Did You Know??
If there is no woman in the house to light the candles, then a man or boy lights them.

A Closer Look
The Shabbos and Yom Tov candles add brightness and joy to the home.

תִּקְעוּ / Tik'u

At *Maariv* on each night of Rosh Hashanah, the following verse is said before *Shemoneh Esrei*.

Blow the shofar at the beginning of this new month, at the time of our holiday, because it is a law for Jewish people to do so, a Judgment Day for Hashem.

תִּקְעוּ בַחֹדֶשׁ שׁוֹפָר, בַּכֶּסֶה לְיוֹם חַגֵּנוּ, כִּי חֹק לְיִשְׂרָאֵל הוּא, מִשְׁפָּט לֵאלֹהֵי יַעֲקֹב.

A Closer Look
Rosh Hashanah is the day when Hashem judges the world.

Did You Know??
The Torah calls Rosh Hashanah "*Yom Teru'ah*," the day of the blowing of the shofar.

A Closer Look
The Torah teaches us that we are commanded by Hashem to blow the shofar on Rosh Hashanah, when the month of Tishrei begins.

Did You Know??
Our Sages give us many reasons to help us understand the mitzvah of blowing the shofar on Rosh Hashanah. Some of them are:

1. The shofar used to be blown when a new king was anointed. We blow the shofar to show that we accept Hashem's Kingship over us on Rosh Hashanah.

2. The sound of the shofar awakens us to repent.

3. It reminds us of the ram that Avraham sacrificed in place of his own son, Yitzchak.

4. It reminds us of the shofar that was heard at Har Sinai when the Torah was given.

5. It reminds us that one day *Mashiach* will come and the Great Shofar will be blown.

Did You Know??
We blow the shofar twice, once before *Mussaf* and again during the *Mussaf Shemoneh Esrei*. This confuses Satan so that he will not be able to make evil claims about us when we are being judged by Hashem.

A Closer Look
Once, shortly before Rosh Hashanah, a man began quickly running out of the *Beis Midrash*. "Where are you going? What is your rush?" asked the Rav.

"I am the *chazzan* for Rosh Hashanah, and I must look through the *machzor* to get my prayers in order," the man replied.

"The *machzor* is no different than it was last year," explained the Rav. "It would be better if you looked at your own actions and put those in order first."

לְשָׁנָה טוֹבָה / Leshanah Tovah

On the night of Rosh Hashanah after we finish davening, we wish other people a healthy and happy New Year with the following words. Even though in English the greeting is the same for men and women, in Hebrew grammar the greetings for men and women are different.

To a man: May you be written and your fate sealed for a good year (right away).

זכר: לְשָׁנָה טוֹבָה תִּכָּתֵב וְתֵחָתֵם (לְאַלְתַּר, לְחַיִּים טוֹבִים וּלְשָׁלוֹם).

To a woman: May you be written and your fate sealed for a good year (right away).

לנקבה: לְשָׁנָה טוֹבָה תִּכָּתֵבִי וְתֵחָתֵמִי (לְאַלְתַּר, לְחַיִּים טוֹבִים וּלְשָׁלוֹם).

To many men: May all of you be written and your fates sealed for a good year (right away).

לזכרים: לְשָׁנָה טוֹבָה תִּכָּתֵבוּ וְתֵחָתֵמוּ (לְאַלְתַּר, לְחַיִּים טוֹבִים וּלְשָׁלוֹם).

To many women: May all of you be written and your fates sealed for a good year (right away).

לנקבות: לְשָׁנָה טוֹבָה תִּכָּתַבְנָה וְתֵחָתַמְנָה (לְאַלְתַּר, לְחַיִּים טוֹבִים וּלְשָׁלוֹם).

Did You Know??
On Rosh Hashanah Hashem opens three books: One book is for the totally righteous people, one book is for the totally wicked people, and one book is for the people in between. The righteous and wicked are inscribed in their books right away and their judgment is sealed. But the book for the people in between (which is most of us) is not sealed until Yom Kippur. This gives us extra time to repent.

Did You Know??
Our Sages teach us that many important "firsts" happened in Tishrei: Hashem created the world, some of our *Avos* (our forefathers) were born, and Yosef was freed from prison in Egypt.

A Closer Look
The Jewish New Year is celebrated very differently from the non-Jewish New Year. On the non-Jewish New Year people make parties and celebrations. The Jewish New Year, on the other hand, is a time when we pray to Hashem and declare that He is our King. It is a time of year when we look deeply into our actions.

A Closer Look
After wishing everyone a good year, we go home joyfully without any sadness. This is because we are confident that Hashem will decree a good year for us.

סִימָנִים / *Simanim*

On the first night of Rosh Hashanah we dip the challah into honey.
After eating the challah, we dip a piece of apple into honey and say the following *berachah*:

Blessed are You, Hashem, our God, King of the universe, Who creates the fruit of the tree.

בָּרוּךְ אַתָּה יהוה אֱלֹהֵינוּ מֶלֶךְ הָעוֹלָם, בּוֹרֵא פְּרִי הָעֵץ.

We eat a piece of the apple and say the following prayer before finishing the apple:

Let it be Your Will, Hashem, our God, the God of our fathers, that you renew us for a good and sweet year.

יְהִי רָצוֹן מִלְּפָנֶיךָ, יהוה אֱלֹהֵינוּ וֵאלֹהֵי אֲבוֹתֵינוּ, שֶׁתְּחַדֵּשׁ עָלֵינוּ שָׁנָה טוֹבָה וּמְתוּקָה.

It is customary for many people to eat the following foods on Rosh Hashanah, and say these prayers when the food is eaten:

for carrots (*rubya* — Aramaic for carrots):

Let it be Your Will, Hashem, our God, the God of our fathers, that our merits increase (*sheyirbu*).

יְהִי רָצוֹן מִלְּפָנֶיךָ, יהוה אֱלֹהֵינוּ וֵאלֹהֵי אֲבוֹתֵינוּ, שֶׁיִּרְבּוּ זְכֻיּוֹתֵינוּ.

for leek (*karsi* — Aramaic for leeks):

Let it be Your Will, Hashem, our God, the God of our fathers, that those who hate us be cut away (*yikarsu*).

יְהִי רָצוֹן מִלְּפָנֶיךָ, יהוה אֱלֹהֵינוּ וֵאלֹהֵי אֲבוֹתֵינוּ, שֶׁיִּכָּרְתוּ שׂוֹנְאֵינוּ.

for beets (*selek* — Aramaic for beets):

Let it be Your Will, Hashem, our God, the God of our fathers, that our enemies be taken away (*yistalku*).

יְהִי רָצוֹן מִלְּפָנֶיךָ, יהוה אֱלֹהֵינוּ וֵאלֹהֵי אֲבוֹתֵינוּ, שֶׁיִּסְתַּלְּקוּ אוֹיְבֵינוּ.

Did You Know??
We eat sweet foods on Rosh Hashanah in the hope that we will have a sweet year.

A Closer Look
The names of the foods should remind us to pray to Hashem to help us.

10

for dates (tamar — Hebrew for dates):

Let it be Your Will, Hashem, our God, the God of our fathers, that those who hate us be demolished (*yitamu*).

יְהִי רָצוֹן מִלְּפָנֶיךָ, יהוה אֱלֹהֵינוּ וֵאלֹהֵי אֲבוֹתֵינוּ, שֶׁיִּתַּמּוּ שׂוֹנְאֵינוּ.

for pomegranate:

Let it be Your Will, Hashem, our God, the God of our fathers, that our merits be numerous like the seeds of the pomegranate.

יְהִי רָצוֹן מִלְּפָנֶיךָ, יהוה אֱלֹהֵינוּ וֵאלֹהֵי אֲבוֹתֵינוּ, שֶׁנַּרְבֶּה זְכִיּוֹת כְּרִמּוֹן.

for fish:

Let it be Your Will, Hashem, our God, the God of our fathers, that we be fruitful and multiply like fish.

יְהִי רָצוֹן מִלְּפָנֶיךָ, יהוה אֱלֹהֵינוּ וֵאלֹהֵי אֲבוֹתֵינוּ, שֶׁנִּפְרֶה וְנִרְבֶּה כְּדָגִים.

for the head of a sheep or head of a fish:

Let it be Your Will, Hashem, our God, the God of our fathers, that we be the head and not the tail.

יְהִי רָצוֹן מִלְּפָנֶיךָ, יהוה אֱלֹהֵינוּ וֵאלֹהֵי אֲבוֹתֵינוּ, שֶׁנִּהְיֶה לְרֹאשׁ וְלֹא לְזָנָב.

Did You Know??

There is a custom not to eat sour or bitter foods on Rosh Hashanah, because we do not want "bitter" or unhappy things to happen to us . Also, some people do not eat nuts on Rosh Hashanah. This is because the number value (*gematria*) of the word "nuts" (*egoz*) is seventeen; the same *gematria* as the word *cheit*, which means "sin."

Did You Know??

The names of each of these foods remind us of a word in Hebrew or Aramaic that we turn into a prayer. For example, we eat beets (*selek* in Aramaic) and we say "*sheyistalku oyveinu* — that our enemies be taken away." A pomegranate is filled with many seeds. When we eat a pomegranate, we ask that our merits be very numerous, just like the seeds of a pomegranate.

Mishnayos of Rosh Hashanah

Some have a custom to study *Mishnayos Rosh Hashanah* on Rosh Hashanah.
Mishnayos Rosh Hashanah talks about a number of subjects related to the New Year,
including declaring the new month each month.
This is a summary of the nine Mishnahs in the first chapter of *Mishnayos Rosh Hashanah*.

[1] There are four different new years for four different cycles in the calendar.

[2] There are four times of the year when the world is judged for different things. On the first day of Tishrei, every person is judged.

[3] Six times during the year the Jewish Court sent messengers to tell Jewish communities which day the Court declared Rosh Chodesh. That way people will know when the Jewish holidays will occur.

[4] People who saw the new moon can sometimes travel to the Court even on Shabbos, in order to tell the Court that they saw the moon.

Did You Know??

The Mishnah was arranged by Rabbi Yehudah HaNasi, together with the other Rabbis of his time, about 1900 years ago. It is a collection of Jewish laws and ethics that explain the Written Torah that was given to Moshe Rabbeinu at Har Sinai. All the teachings of the Mishnah and Gemara were taught to Moshe when he received the Torah.

A Closer Look

In the olden times, there was no calendar. *Beis Din*, the Rabbinic Court, had to decide, based on witnesses seeing the new moon, if the month was 29 or 30 days.

[5] The witnesses may travel on Shabbos even if they saw the moon on a clear night, even though we can assume that other people, who lived near the Court, had probably seen the moon also.

[6] Once, more than forty pairs of witnesses were on their way to Yerushalayim to testify that it was the beginning of a new month. Since there were so many people, Rabbi Akiva told most of them that they need not travel to Yerushalayim. Rabban Gamliel said that it is not good to tell the people that they are not needed, because they may decide not to make the trip a different time, when they would be needed.

Mishnayos 7-9 discuss details of who may be witnesses and the laws of their traveling on Shabbos.

הַמֶּלֶךְ / HaMelech

The King

sits upon a high and exalted Throne.

הַמֶּלֶךְ
יוֹשֵׁב עַל כִּסֵּא רָם וְנִשָּׂא.

Did You Know??

On a regular Shabbos or Yom Tov the *chazzan* begins this part of davening with the words שׁוֹכֵן עַד. But on Rosh Hashanah, when Hashem is sitting on His heavenly Throne and judging the Jewish people, he begins several words earlier, with the word הַמֶּלֶךְ, the King Who sits on His Throne.

A Closer Look

In most congregations, the *chazzan* stays in his place in Shul, and gradually raises his voice as he begins to sing the traditional tune. He finally sings out in a loud voice, "*HaMelech*!" He then slowly walks up to the *amud* and continues from there. The commentaries tell us that this prayer has a mystical effect. It is able to chase away from Hashem's Throne of Glory the angels that are making accusations against the Jewish people.

HaMelech means THE King. If we would only fully realize and understand that Hashem is really THE King over all kings — if only we would be afraid of Him as much as we are afraid of a king or ruler who is only human!

Once, when R' Aharon of Karlin called out "*HaMelech*," he fainted. He explained, "When R' Yochanan ben Zakkai appeared before Vespasian, who had just become emperor of Rome, R' Yochanan said, 'May you have peace, our king.'

"'If you know I am king,' answered Vespasian, 'why have you waited so long to come to me?' "

R' Aharon then cried and said, "Woe is me that it has taken me so long to come before Hashem, declare that He is the King, and properly do *teshuvah*."

R' Yochanan ben Zakkai meets Vespasian

שִׁיר הַמַּעֲלוֹת / Shir Hama'alos Perek 130

A song that the Leviim used to sing on the steps of the *Beis HaMikdash*: From deep troubles I called to You, Hashem. My Master, listen to what I say; please hear what I am begging for. If You keep all our sins, who would survive? You can forgive our sins, so we fear You. I trust in You, Hashem, I long to hear You. My soul yearns for You, Hashem, more than the night-watchman waits for the morning. Let Israel hope for Hashem, because Hashem is kind, and great salvation is with Him. He will save Israel from all its sins.

שִׁיר הַמַּעֲלוֹת, מִמַּעֲמַקִּים קְרָאתִיךָ, יְהוָה. אֲדֹנָי, שִׁמְעָה בְקוֹלִי, תִּהְיֶינָה אָזְנֶיךָ קַשֻּׁבוֹת לְקוֹל תַּחֲנוּנָי. אִם עֲוֺנוֹת תִּשְׁמָר יָהּ, אֲדֹנָי מִי יַעֲמֹד. כִּי עִמְּךָ הַסְּלִיחָה, לְמַעַן תִּוָּרֵא. קִוִּיתִי יְהוָה, קִוְּתָה נַפְשִׁי, וְלִדְבָרוֹ הוֹחָלְתִּי. נַפְשִׁי לַאדֹנָי, מִשֹּׁמְרִים לַבֹּקֶר, שֹׁמְרִים לַבֹּקֶר. יַחֵל יִשְׂרָאֵל אֶל יְהוָה, כִּי עִם יְהוָה הַחֶסֶד, וְהַרְבֵּה עִמּוֹ פְדוּת. וְהוּא יִפְדֶּה אֶת יִשְׂרָאֵל, מִכֹּל עֲוֺנוֹתָיו.

Shema Yisrael is said here (see page 65)

A Closer Look

This prayer is taken from the Book of *Tehillim*. One of the purposes of *Tehillim* is to raise our spirits when we are sad. This chapter of *Tehillim* teaches us that no matter how bad things look, Hashem can save us. For Hashem, nothing is impossible; everything can be done. We learn here that we should return to Hashem, ask Him for forgiveness, and trust that He can help.

First Berachos of Shemoneh Esrei
Rosh Hashanah and Yom Kippur

Shemoneh Esrei is the most important part of our prayers, all year. It is also the highlight of our prayers on Rosh Hashanah and Yom Kippur. We first take three steps backward and then three steps forward. It is as if we are coming closer to Hashem, the King. We stand with our feet together during the entire *Shemoneh Esrei*.

> At *Minchah* we add this verse:
>
> כִּי שֵׁם יהוה אֶקְרָא, הָבוּ גֹדֶל לֵאלֹהֵינוּ.
>
> When I call out the Name of Hashem, I speak greatness of our God.

At all Tefillos:

My Lord, open my lips so I can praise You.　　　אֲדֹנָי שְׂפָתַי תִּפְתָּח, וּפִי יַגִּיד תְּהִלָּתֶךָ.

Berachah 1: אָבוֹת / Fathers

In the first *berachah* we speak about Hashem's greatness and how He guided our forefathers.
Our Sages tell us that we must take special care to concentrate on the meaning of this first *berachah*.
In this *berachah* we bend our knees when we say בָּרוּך, and we bow when we say אַתָּה.
Then we stand up straight before we say the Name of Hashem.

Blessed are You, Hashem, our God and the God of our fathers, the God of Avraham, the God of Yitzchak, and the God of Yaakov, the great, mighty, powerful, and supreme God; Who is kind and owns everything, Who remembers the good deeds of our fathers, and brings *Mashiach* to their grandchildren, for His sake, with love.

בָּרוּךְ אַתָּה יהוה אֱלֹהֵינוּ וֵאלֹהֵי אֲבוֹתֵינוּ, אֱלֹהֵי אַבְרָהָם, אֱלֹהֵי יִצְחָק, וֵאלֹהֵי יַעֲקֹב, הָאֵל הַגָּדוֹל הַגִּבּוֹר וְהַנּוֹרָא, אֵל עֶלְיוֹן, גּוֹמֵל חֲסָדִים טוֹבִים, וְקוֹנֵה הַכֹּל, וְזוֹכֵר חַסְדֵי אָבוֹת, וּמֵבִיא גוֹאֵל לִבְנֵי בְנֵיהֶם, לְמַעַן שְׁמוֹ בְּאַהֲבָה.

Did You Know??
When we pray, we are like the *Avos*: Avraham, Yitzchak, and Yaakov. They were the first people to pray *Shacharis*, *Minchah*, and *Maariv*.

Did You Know??
When we say *Shemoneh Esrei*, we should stand with our feet together. Our Sages teach us that we should keep our feet together when praying so that we will be similar to angels , who appear to have one straight leg.

Remember us for life, King Who wants life. Write us in the Book of Life — for Your sake.

זָכְרֵנוּ לְחַיִּים, מֶלֶךְ חָפֵץ בַּחַיִּים, וְכָתְבֵנוּ בְּסֵפֶר הַחַיִּים, לְמַעַנְךָ אֱלֹהִים חַיִּים.

We now again bend our knees when we say **בָּרוּךְ**, and we bow when we say **אַתָּה**.

You are the King, Who saves us and helps and protects us. Blessed are You, Hashem, the protector of Avraham.

מֶלֶךְ עוֹזֵר וּמוֹשִׁיעַ וּמָגֵן. בָּרוּךְ אַתָּה יהוה, מָגֵן אַבְרָהָם.

Berachah 2: גְּבוּרוֹת / God's Power

In the second *berachah* we praise Hashem for His mighty deeds, including that when *Mashiach* comes, Hashem will bring the dead back to life.

You are powerful forever, my Lord. You bring the dead back to life, You are able to save.

אַתָּה גִּבּוֹר לְעוֹלָם, אֲדֹנָי, מְחַיֵּה מֵתִים אַתָּה, רַב לְהוֹשִׁיעַ.

People who daven Nusach Sefard and people in Eretz Yisrael add:

You make the dew fall.

מוֹרִיד הַטָּל.

You keep us alive with kindness. You bring the dead back to life. You support those who fall. You heal the sick. You free the prisoners. And You keep Your promise to the dead (to bring them back to life). Who is like You, our King, Who causes people to die, and brings them back to life, and Who makes salvation grow.

מְכַלְכֵּל חַיִּים בְּחֶסֶד, מְחַיֵּה מֵתִים בְּרַחֲמִים רַבִּים, סוֹמֵךְ נוֹפְלִים, וְרוֹפֵא חוֹלִים, וּמַתִּיר אֲסוּרִים, וּמְקַיֵּם אֱמוּנָתוֹ לִישֵׁנֵי עָפָר. מִי כָמוֹךָ בַּעַל גְּבוּרוֹת, וּמִי דוֹמֶה לָךְ, מֶלֶךְ מֵמִית וּמְחַיֶּה וּמַצְמִיחַ יְשׁוּעָה.

From Rosh Hashanah to Yom Kippur, we add:

Who is like You, Father of mercy, Who remembers everyone in order that they live!

מִי כָמוֹךָ אַב הָרַחֲמִים, זוֹכֵר יְצוּרָיו לְחַיִּים בְּרַחֲמִים.

We trust you to bring the dead back to life. Blessed are You, Hashem, Who brings the dead back to life!

וְנֶאֱמָן אַתָּה לְהַחֲיוֹת מֵתִים. בָּרוּךְ אַתָּה יהוה, מְחַיֵּה הַמֵּתִים.

Did You Know??
When we recite the *Shemoneh Esrei*, we are speaking directly to Hashem, begging Him to help us. That is why we take three steps backward and three steps forward, as if we are walking up to His throne. Nowhere else in davening is this done.

A Closer Look
Unlike the *Shemoneh Esrei* prayer during the rest of the year, on Rosh Hashanah we stress two special ideas. First we speak about the special status of the Jewish People as Hashem's Chosen People. Secondly we constantly speak about Hashem being our King and judging us.

Berachah 3:
קְדוּשַׁת הַשֵּׁם / The Holiness of Hashem

אַתָּה קָדוֹשׁ וְשִׁמְךָ קָדוֹשׁ, וּקְדוֹשִׁים בְּכָל יוֹם יְהַלְלוּךָ סֶּלָה.

You are holy and Your Name is holy, and holy ones praise You every day, forever.

וּבְכֵן, תֵּן פַּחְדְּךָ, יהוה אֱלֹהֵינוּ, עַל כָּל מַעֲשֶׂיךָ, וְאֵימָתְךָ עַל כָּל מַה שֶּׁבָּרָאתָ. וְיִירָאוּךָ כָּל הַמַּעֲשִׂים, וְיִשְׁתַּחֲווּ לְפָנֶיךָ כָּל הַבְּרוּאִים. וְיֵעָשׂוּ כֻלָּם אֲגֻדָּה אַחַת לַעֲשׂוֹת רְצוֹנְךָ בְּלֵבָב שָׁלֵם. כְּמוֹ שֶׁיָּדַעְנוּ, יהוה אֱלֹהֵינוּ, שֶׁהַשָּׁלְטָן לְפָנֶיךָ, עֹז בְּיָדְךָ, וּגְבוּרָה בִּימִינֶךָ, וְשִׁמְךָ נוֹרָא עַל כָּל מַה שֶּׁבָּרָאתָ.

And so, also, Hashem, our God, let all Your creations fear You, and be in awe of You. Let all Your creations fear You and bow down before You. Let them all unite and join together to do Your Will. We know that everything is Yours, You are all-powerful, and Your Name brings fear into everything that You have created.

Did You Know??
Nothing is greater or stronger than the power of prayer.

Did You Know??
When we pray for others, our prayers for ourselves are answered more quickly.

וּבְכֵן, תֵּן כָּבוֹד, יהוה, לְעַמֶּךָ, תְּהִלָּה לִירֵאֶיךָ, וְתִקְוָה טוֹבָה לְדוֹרְשֶׁיךָ, וּפִתְחוֹן פֶּה לַמְיַחֲלִים לָךְ, שִׂמְחָה לְאַרְצֶךָ, וְשָׂשׂוֹן לְעִירֶךָ, וּצְמִיחַת קֶרֶן לְדָוִד עַבְדֶּךָ, וַעֲרִיכַת נֵר לְבֶן יִשַׁי מְשִׁיחֶךָ, בִּמְהֵרָה בְיָמֵינוּ.

And so, also, Hashem, our God, give honor to Your nation, and praise to those who fear You. Give hope to those who seek You; and let those who hope to You be able to speak proudly; bring happiness to Your Land, and joy to Your city, Yerushalayim. Prepare the way for the *Mashiach*, the descendant of King David, to come quickly in our time.

וּבְכֵן, צַדִּיקִים יִרְאוּ וְיִשְׂמָחוּ, וִישָׁרִים יַעֲלֹזוּ, וַחֲסִידִים בְּרִנָּה יָגִילוּ. וְעוֹלָתָה תִּקְפָּץ פִּיהָ, וְכָל הָרִשְׁעָה כֻּלָּהּ כְּעָשָׁן תִּכְלֶה, כִּי תַעֲבִיר מֶמְשֶׁלֶת זָדוֹן מִן הָאָרֶץ.

And so, also, the *tzaddikim* will then see and be happy, and they will sing with joy. Sin will be quiet, and all things wicked will blow away like smoke, when You will take away the power of wickedness from the world.

Did You Know??
When *Mashiach* comes, everyone in the world will join in praising Hashem. This is what we are praying for in this *berachah*.

A Closer Look
When Jews pray together, they become one united people.

Then You, Hashem, will rule over all Your creations, on Har Tziyon, the resting place of Your *Shechinah*, in Yerushalayim, Your holy city. As it is written in *Sefer Tehillim*, Hashem will rule forever, from generation to generation. Halleluyah.

וְתִמְלוֹךְ אַתָּה יהוה לְבַדֶּךָ, עַל כָּל מַעֲשֶׂיךָ, בְּהַר צִיּוֹן מִשְׁכַּן כְּבוֹדֶךָ, וּבִירוּשָׁלַיִם עִיר קָדְשֶׁךָ, כַּכָּתוּב בְּדִבְרֵי קָדְשֶׁךָ: יִמְלֹךְ יהוה לְעוֹלָם, אֱלֹהַיִךְ צִיּוֹן לְדֹר וָדֹר, הַלְלוּיָהּ.

You are holy and Your Name is full of fear. There is no god other than You, as it is written [in *Sefer Yeshayahu*], Hashem, Master of the armies, will be exalted in judgment, and the holy God will be made holy in righteousness. Blessed are You, Hashem, the holy King.

קָדוֹשׁ אַתָּה וְנוֹרָא שְׁמֶךָ, וְאֵין אֱלוֹהַּ מִבַּלְעָדֶיךָ, כַּכָּתוּב: וַיִּגְבַּהּ יהוה צְבָאוֹת בַּמִּשְׁפָּט, וְהָאֵל הַקָּדוֹשׁ נִקְדַּשׁ בִּצְדָקָה. בָּרוּךְ אַתָּה יהוה, הַמֶּלֶךְ הַקָּדוֹשׁ.

Did You Know??
On Rosh Hashanah, and until after Yom Kippur, we refer to Hashem in this *berachah* as the Holy *King*, in contrast to the Holy *God*.

לְקֵל עוֹרֵךְ דִּין / L'Keil Oreich Din

Many congregations say this at *Shacharis* on the first day; and at *Mussaf* on the second day.

To Hashem: And so everyone will crown You Who prepares us to be judged.

וּבְכֵן לְךָ הַכֹּל יַכְתִּירוּ

To Hashem, Who prepares man for judgment;

לְאֵל עוֹרֵךְ דִּין.

To the One Who sees inside man's heart on the day of judgment;

לְבוֹחֵן לְבָבוֹת בְּיוֹם דִּין.

To the One Who shows what is deep in man's heart, in judgment;

לְגוֹלֶה עֲמוּקוֹת בַּדִּין.

To the One Who speaks only in truth on the day of judgment;

לְדוֹבֵר מֵישָׁרִים בְּיוֹם דִּין.

To the One Who understands our thoughts, in judgment;

לְהוֹגֶה דֵעוֹת בַּדִּין.

To the Ancient One Who does kindness on the day of judgment;

לְוָתִיק וְעֹשֶׂה חֶסֶד בְּיוֹם דִּין.

A Closer Look

This prayer starts with the words "To Hashem, Who prepares man for judgment." This means that Hashem has shown us how to repent and make ourselves better. When we do that, we can ask Him to forgive our sins. We just have to do our part. Then we can ask Him for forgiveness.

Did You Know??

It is customary to wake up early to go to shul on Rosh Hashanah. There are five times during the year when we should get up especially early to go to shul: Rosh Hashanah, Yom Kippur, Hoshana Rabbah, Purim, and Tishah B'Av. The last letter of each of these holidays spells out the name *Avraham*. The Torah teaches us that Avraham "got up early in the morning" to serve Hashem (*Bereishis* 19:27).

English		Hebrew
To the One Who remembers His agreement with the Jewish people in judgment;	בַּדִּין.	לְזוֹכֵר בְּרִיתוֹ
To the One Who has compassion on His creations on the day of judgment;	בְּיוֹם דִּין.	לְחוֹמֵל מַעֲשָׂיו
To the One Who purifies those who trust in Him, in judgment;	בַּדִּין.	לְטַהֵר חוֹסָיו
To the One Who knows everyone's thoughts on the day of judgment;	בְּיוֹם דִּין.	לְיוֹדֵעַ מַחֲשָׁבוֹת
To the One Who holds back His anger in judgment;	בַּדִּין.	לְכוֹבֵשׁ כַּעֲסוֹ
To the One Who shows His righteousness on the day of judgment;	בְּיוֹם דִּין.	לְלוֹבֵשׁ צְדָקוֹת
To the One Who forgives sins in judgment;	בַּדִּין.	לְמוֹחֵל עֲוֹנוֹת
To the One Who is too great to be praised on the day of judgment;	בְּיוֹם דִּין.	לְנוֹרָא תְהִלּוֹת
To the One Who forgives His people in judgment;	בַּדִּין.	לְסוֹלֵחַ לַעֲמוּסָיו
To the One Who answers those who call to Him on the day of judgment;	בְּיוֹם דִּין.	לְעוֹנֶה לְקוֹרְאָיו
To the One Who is merciful in judgment;	בַּדִּין.	לְפוֹעֵל רַחֲמָיו
To the One Who sees what is hidden on the day of judgment;	בְּיוֹם דִּין.	לְצוֹפֶה נִסְתָּרוֹת
To the One Who claims His servants in judgment;	בַּדִּין.	לְקוֹנֶה עֲבָדָיו
To the One Who shows mercy to His people on the day of judgment;	בְּיוֹם דִּין.	לְרַחֵם עַמּוֹ
To the One Who watches over His beloved people in judgment;	בַּדִּין.	לְשׁוֹמֵר אוֹהֲבָיו
To the One Who supports His pure people on the day of judgment.	בְּיוֹם דִּין.	לְתוֹמֵךְ תְּמִימָיו

אָבִינוּ מַלְכֵּנוּ / *Avinu Malkeinu*

Many congregations say this at *Shacharis* on the first day; and at *Mussaf*, on the second day.

Our Father, our King, we have sinned before You.

אָבִינוּ מַלְכֵּנוּ, חָטָאנוּ לְפָנֶיךָ.

Our Father, our King, we have no other King, just You.

אָבִינוּ מַלְכֵּנוּ, אֵין לָנוּ מֶלֶךְ אֶלָּא אָתָּה.

Our Father, our King, be kind to us for the sake of Your Name.

אָבִינוּ מַלְכֵּנוּ, עֲשֵׂה עִמָּנוּ לְמַעַן שְׁמֶךָ.

Our Father, our King, renew us for a good year.

אָבִינוּ מַלְכֵּנוּ, חַדֵּשׁ עָלֵינוּ שָׁנָה טוֹבָה.

Our Father, our King, eliminate all bad decrees written against us.

אָבִינוּ מַלְכֵּנוּ, בַּטֵּל מֵעָלֵינוּ כָּל גְּזֵרוֹת קָשׁוֹת.

Did You Know??

One year there was no rain in Eretz Yisrael. The people were hungry and thirsty. All the great rabbis prayed to Hashem for rain and also told the people to pray as hard as they could. But no rain fell. Then Rabbi Akiva went up to the *Aron Kodesh* in the shul and recited the prayer אָבִינוּ מַלְכֵּנוּ, "Our Father, our King, we have no other King, just You. Our Father our King, for Your Sake, have mercy on us." And the rain immediately fell.

Did You Know??

We say the verses "Our Father, our King, write us in the book of ... five times." These five times correspond to the Torah, the Five Books of Moses; the first time to *Bereishis*, the second time to *Shemos*, and so on.

Our Father, our King, eliminate all bad thoughts of those who hate us.	אָבִינוּ מַלְכֵּנוּ, בַּטֵּל מַחְשְׁבוֹת שׂוֹנְאֵינוּ.
Our Father, our King, change the evil plans of our enemies.	אָבִינוּ מַלְכֵּנוּ, הָפֵר עֲצַת אוֹיְבֵינוּ.
Our Father, our King, get rid of all our enemies and those who want to stop us.	אָבִינוּ מַלְכֵּנוּ, כַּלֵּה כָּל צַר וּמַשְׂטִין מֵעָלֵינוּ.
Our Father, our King, seal the mouths of anyone who accuses us.	אָבִינוּ מַלְכֵּנוּ, סְתוֹם פִּיּוֹת מַשְׂטִינֵנוּ וּמְקַטְרִיגֵנוּ.
Our Father, our King, eliminate disease, killing, hunger, captivity, destruction, and sin from Your people.	אָבִינוּ מַלְכֵּנוּ, כַּלֵּה דֶּבֶר וְחֶרֶב וְרָעָב וּשְׁבִי וּמַשְׁחִית וְעָוֹן וּשְׁמַד מִבְּנֵי בְרִיתֶךָ.
Our Father, our King, keep plagues away from us.	אָבִינוּ מַלְכֵּנוּ, מְנַע מַגֵּפָה מִנַּחֲלָתֶךָ.
Our Father, our King, forgive all our sins.	אָבִינוּ מַלְכֵּנוּ, סְלַח וּמְחַל לְכָל עֲוֹנוֹתֵינוּ.
Our Father, our King, wipe away our intentional sins and mistakes.	אָבִינוּ מַלְכֵּנוּ, מְחֵה וְהַעֲבֵר פְּשָׁעֵינוּ וְחַטֹּאתֵינוּ מִנֶּגֶד עֵינֶיךָ.
Our Father, our King, through Your kindness, erase all our guilt.	אָבִינוּ מַלְכֵּנוּ, מְחוֹק בְּרַחֲמֶיךָ הָרַבִּים כָּל שִׁטְרֵי חוֹבוֹתֵינוּ.

Each of the nine verses is said first by the *chazzan* and then repeated by the congregation.

Our Father, our King, return us to You with perfect repentance.	אָבִינוּ מַלְכֵּנוּ, הַחֲזִירֵנוּ בִּתְשׁוּבָה שְׁלֵמָה לְפָנֶיךָ.
Our Father, our King, heal the sick with a complete recovery.	אָבִינוּ מַלְכֵּנוּ, שְׁלַח רְפוּאָה שְׁלֵמָה לְחוֹלֵי עַמֶּךָ.
Our Father, our King, tear up any evil decrees against us.	אָבִינוּ מַלְכֵּנוּ, קְרַע רוֹעַ גְּזַר דִּינֵנוּ.
Our Father, our King, remember us for good.	אָבִינוּ מַלְכֵּנוּ, זָכְרֵנוּ בְּזִכָּרוֹן טוֹב לְפָנֶיךָ.
Our Father, our King, write us in the book of good life.	אָבִינוּ מַלְכֵּנוּ, כָּתְבֵנוּ בְּסֵפֶר חַיִּים טוֹבִים.
Our Father, our King, write us in the book of redemption and salvation.	אָבִינוּ מַלְכֵּנוּ, כָּתְבֵנוּ בְּסֵפֶר גְּאֻלָּה וִישׁוּעָה.

Our Father, our King, write us in the book of sustenance and support.

אָבִינוּ מַלְכֵּנוּ, כָּתְבֵנוּ בְּסֵפֶר פַּרְנָסָה וְכַלְכָּלָה.

Our Father, our King, write us in the book of merits.

אָבִינוּ מַלְכֵּנוּ, כָּתְבֵנוּ בְּסֵפֶר זְכֻיּוֹת.

Our Father, our King, write us in the book of forgiveness.

אָבִינוּ מַלְכֵּנוּ, כָּתְבֵנוּ בְּסֵפֶר סְלִיחָה וּמְחִילָה.

The congregation and the *chazzan* continue saying to themselves the following verses.

Our Father, our King, let our salvation sprout like a plant, very soon.

אָבִינוּ מַלְכֵּנוּ, הַצְמַח לָנוּ יְשׁוּעָה בְּקָרוֹב.

Our Father, our King, lift up the pride of Your people.

אָבִינוּ מַלְכֵּנוּ, הָרֵם קֶרֶן יִשְׂרָאֵל עַמֶּךָ.

Our Father, our King, lift up the pride of Your *Mashiach*.

אָבִינוּ מַלְכֵּנוּ, הָרֵם קֶרֶן מְשִׁיחֶךָ.

Our Father, our King, fill our hands with Your blessings.

אָבִינוּ מַלְכֵּנוּ, מַלֵּא יָדֵינוּ מִבִּרְכוֹתֶיךָ.

Our Father, our King, fill up our houses with plenty.

אָבִינוּ מַלְכֵּנוּ, מַלֵּא אֲסָמֵינוּ שָׂבָע.

Our Father, our King, listen to us, and have pity on us.

אָבִינוּ מַלְכֵּנוּ, שְׁמַע קוֹלֵנוּ, חוּס וְרַחֵם עָלֵינוּ.

Our Father, our King, accept our prayers with kindness and mercy.

אָבִינוּ מַלְכֵּנוּ, קַבֵּל בְּרַחֲמִים וּבְרָצוֹן אֶת תְּפִלָּתֵנוּ.

Our Father, our King, open the gates of heaven to our prayer.

אָבִינוּ מַלְכֵּנוּ, פְּתַח שַׁעֲרֵי שָׁמַיִם לִתְפִלָּתֵנוּ.

Our Father, our King, remember that we are only dust.

אָבִינוּ מַלְכֵּנוּ, זְכוֹר כִּי עָפָר אֲנָחְנוּ.

Our Father, our King, please do not make us leave empty-handed.

אָבִינוּ מַלְכֵּנוּ, נָא אַל תְּשִׁיבֵנוּ רֵיקָם מִלְּפָנֶיךָ.

Our Father, our King, may right now be a time of compassion before You.

אָבִינוּ מַלְכֵּנוּ, תְּהֵא הַשָּׁעָה הַזֹּאת שְׁעַת רַחֲמִים וְעֵת רָצוֹן מִלְּפָנֶיךָ.

Our Father, our King, take pity upon us and upon our children and babies.

אָבִינוּ מַלְכֵּנוּ, חֲמוֹל עָלֵינוּ וְעַל עוֹלָלֵינוּ וְטַפֵּנוּ.

Our Father, our King, do it for those who were killed for Your sake.

אָבִינוּ מַלְכֵּנוּ, עֲשֵׂה לְמַעַן הֲרוּגִים עַל שֵׁם קָדְשֶׁךָ.

Our Father, our King, do it for those who were killed for believing that You are One.

אָבִינוּ מַלְכֵּנוּ, עֲשֵׂה לְמַעַן טְבוּחִים עַל יִחוּדֶךָ.

Our Father, our King, do it for those who went into fire and water for Your sake.

אָבִינוּ מַלְכֵּנוּ, עֲשֵׂה לְמַעַן בָּאֵי בָאֵשׁ וּבַמַּיִם עַל קִדּוּשׁ שְׁמֶךָ.

Our Father, our King, let us see You take revenge for all those who were killed.

אָבִינוּ מַלְכֵּנוּ, נְקֹם לְעֵינֵינוּ נִקְמַת דַּם עֲבָדֶיךָ הַשָּׁפוּךְ.

Our Father, our King, do it for Your sake, if not for us.

אָבִינוּ מַלְכֵּנוּ, עֲשֵׂה לְמַעַנְךָ אִם לֹא לְמַעֲנֵנוּ.

Our Father, our King, do it for You, and save us.

אָבִינוּ מַלְכֵּנוּ, עֲשֵׂה לְמַעַנְךָ וְהוֹשִׁיעֵנוּ.

Our Father, our King, do it because of Your compassion.

אָבִינוּ מַלְכֵּנוּ, עֲשֵׂה לְמַעַן רַחֲמֶיךָ הָרַבִּים.

Our Father, our King, do it for Your great and mighty Name, that we are known by.

אָבִינוּ מַלְכֵּנוּ, עֲשֵׂה לְמַעַן שִׁמְךָ הַגָּדוֹל הַגִּבּוֹר וְהַנּוֹרָא, שֶׁנִּקְרָא עָלֵינוּ.

Our Father, our King, be kind to us, and answer us, though we have done nothing worthy; treat us with kindness and charity and save us.

אָבִינוּ מַלְכֵּנוּ, חָנֵּנוּ וַעֲנֵנוּ, כִּי אֵין בָּנוּ מַעֲשִׂים, עֲשֵׂה עִמָּנוּ צְדָקָה וָחֶסֶד וְהוֹשִׁיעֵנוּ.

A Closer Look

Avinu — Our Father — and *Malkeinu* — Our King — are two different ways to think of Hashem. We say "Our Father" hoping Hashem will have mercy on us. We say "Our King" understanding that Hashem is our King and rules over us, and decides what will happen to us.

The pleas in *Avinu Malkeinu* are both personal requests for each of us and national requests for all the Jewish People.

קְרִיאַת הַתּוֹרָה–יוֹם רִאשׁוֹן / Torah Reading – First Day

Two Torahs are taken out of the *Aron Kodesh* and the following Torah section is read.

On the first day we read the story of the birth of Yitzchak in *Chumash Bereishis*.

The English beneath the Hebrew text is a concise adaptation of the story.

בראשית: פרק כא

כא - אַ וַיהֹוָה פָּקַד אֶת־שָׂרָה כַּאֲשֶׁר אָמָר וַיַּעַשׂ יְהֹוָה לְשָׂרָה כַּאֲשֶׁר דִּבֵּר: בַּ וַתַּהַר וַתֵּלֶד שָׂרָה לְאַבְרָהָם בֵּן לִזְקֻנָיו לַמּוֹעֵד אֲשֶׁר־דִּבֶּר אֹתוֹ אֱלֹהִים: גַּ וַיִּקְרָא אַבְרָהָם אֶת־שֶׁם־בְּנוֹ הַנּוֹלַד־לוֹ אֲשֶׁר־יָלְדָה־לּוֹ שָׂרָה יִצְחָק: דַּ וַיָּמָל אַבְרָהָם אֶת־יִצְחָק בְּנוֹ בֶּן־שְׁמֹנַת יָמִים כַּאֲשֶׁר צִוָּה אֹתוֹ אֱלֹהִים: לוי - הַ וְאַבְרָהָם בֶּן־מְאַת שָׁנָה בְּהִוָּלֶד לוֹ אֵת יִצְחָק בְּנוֹ: וַ וַתֹּאמֶר שָׂרָה צְחֹק עָשָׂה לִי אֱלֹהִים כָּל־הַשֹּׁמֵעַ יִצְחַק־לִי: זַ וַתֹּאמֶר מִי מִלֵּל לְאַבְרָהָם הֵינִיקָה בָנִים שָׂרָה כִּי־יָלַדְתִּי בֵן לִזְקֻנָיו: חַ וַיִּגְדַּל הַיֶּלֶד וַיִּגָּמַל וַיַּעַשׂ אַבְרָהָם מִשְׁתֶּה גָדוֹל בְּיוֹם הִגָּמֵל אֶת־יִצְחָק: (בשבת: שלישי) טַ וַתֵּרֶא שָׂרָה אֶת־בֶּן־הָגָר הַמִּצְרִית אֲשֶׁר־יָלְדָה לְאַבְרָהָם מְצַחֵק: יַ וַתֹּאמֶר לְאַבְרָהָם גָּרֵשׁ הָאָמָה הַזֹּאת וְאֶת־בְּנָהּ כִּי לֹא יִירַשׁ בֶּן־הָאָמָה הַזֹּאת עִם־בְּנִי עִם־יִצְחָק: יאַ וַיֵּרַע הַדָּבָר מְאֹד בְּעֵינֵי אַבְרָהָם עַל אוֹדֹת בְּנוֹ: יבַ וַיֹּאמֶר אֱלֹהִים אֶל־אַבְרָהָם אַל־יֵרַע בְּעֵינֶיךָ עַל־הַנַּעַר וְעַל־אֲמָתֶךָ כֹּל אֲשֶׁר תֹּאמַר אֵלֶיךָ שָׂרָה שְׁמַע בְּקֹלָהּ כִּי בְיִצְחָק יִקָּרֵא לְךָ זָרַע: שלישי (בשבת:רביעי) יגַ וְגַם אֶת־בֶּן־הָאָמָה לְגוֹי אֲשִׂימֶנּוּ כִּי זַרְעֲךָ הוּא: ידַ וַיַּשְׁכֵּם אַבְרָהָם | בַּבֹּקֶר וַיִּקַּח־לֶחֶם וְחֵמַת מַיִם וַיִּתֵּן אֶל־הָגָר שָׂם עַל־שִׁכְמָהּ וְאֶת־הַיֶּלֶד וַיְשַׁלְּחֶהָ וַתֵּלֶךְ וַתֵּתַע בְּמִדְבַּר בְּאֵר שָׁבַע: טוַ וַיִּכְלוּ הַמַּיִם מִן־הַחֵמֶת וַתַּשְׁלֵךְ אֶת־הַיֶּלֶד תַּחַת אַחַד הַשִּׂיחִם: טזַ וַתֵּלֶךְ וַתֵּשֶׁב לָהּ מִנֶּגֶד הַרְחֵק כִּמְטַחֲוֵי קֶשֶׁת כִּי אָמְרָה אַל־אֶרְאֶה בְּמוֹת הַיָּלֶד וַתֵּשֶׁב מִנֶּגֶד וַתִּשָּׂא אֶת־קֹלָהּ וַתֵּבְךְּ: יזַ וַיִּשְׁמַע אֱלֹהִים אֶת־קוֹל הַנַּעַר וַיִּקְרָא מַלְאַךְ אֱלֹהִים | אֶל־הָגָר מִן־הַשָּׁמַיִם וַיֹּאמֶר לָהּ מַה־לָּךְ הָגָר אַל־תִּירְאִי כִּי־שָׁמַע

Hashem remembered Sarah and she gave birth to a baby boy. Avraham and Sarah were both very old (Avraham was 100 years old, and Sarah was 90). They named their son Yitzchak. When Yitzchak was eight days old, Avraham circumcised him, just as Hashem had commanded. Years later, Avraham made a big party celebrating Yitzchak's maturing.

Sarah realized that their Egyptian servant, Hagar, and her son, Yishmael, were a bad influence on their son, Yitzchak. "Send them away and out of our house," she told Avraham. It was hard for Avraham to do this, but Hashem told him to listen to his wife, Sarah, since the children who will be called "Avraham's children" will come from Yitzchak.

Avraham took bread and water, gave them to Hagar and Yishmael, and sent them away into the desert. After a short while, they ran out of water. Hagar was sure that Yishmael would die. She did not want to see it happen, so she went far away. Hashem sent an angel to show her where to find water. The angel told Hagar, "Do not worry. I will make this boy into a great nation." And Hashem saved them.

אֱלֹהִים אֶל־קוֹל הַנַּעַר בַּאֲשֶׁר הוּא־שָׁם:
(בשבת: חמישי) יח קוּמִי שְׂאִי אֶת־הַנַּעַר וְהַחֲזִיקִי אֶת־
יָדֵךְ בּוֹ כִּי־לְגוֹי גָּדוֹל אֲשִׂימֶנּוּ: יט וַיִּפְקַח אֱלֹהִים
אֶת־עֵינֶיהָ וַתֵּרֶא בְּאֵר מָיִם וַתֵּלֶךְ וַתְּמַלֵּא אֶת־
הַחֵמֶת מַיִם וַתַּשְׁקְ אֶת־הַנָּעַר: כ וַיְהִי אֱלֹהִים

אֶת־הַנַּעַר וַיִּגְדָּל וַיֵּשֶׁב בַּמִּדְבָּר וַיְהִי רֹבֶה קַשָּׁת:
כא וַיֵּשֶׁב בְּמִדְבַּר פָּארָן וַתִּקַּח־לוֹ אִמּוֹ אִשָּׁה
מֵאֶרֶץ מִצְרָיִם:

רביעי (בשבת: ששי) כב וַיְהִי בָּעֵת הַהִוא וַיֹּאמֶר אֲבִימֶלֶךְ
וּפִיכֹל שַׂר־צְבָאוֹ אֶל־אַבְרָהָם לֵאמֹר אֱלֹהִים

עִמְּךָ֒ בְּכֹ֣ל אֲשֶׁר־אַתָּ֖ה עֹשֶֽׂה: כגוְעַתָּ֗ה הִשָּׁ֤בְעָה
לִּי֙ בֵֽאלֹהִים֙ הֵ֔נָּה אִם־תִּשְׁקֹ֣ר לִ֔י וּלְנִינִ֖י וּלְנֶכְדִּ֑י
כַּחֶ֜סֶד אֲשֶׁר־עָשִׂ֤יתִי עִמְּךָ֙ תַּעֲשֶׂ֣ה עִמָּדִ֔י וְעִם־
הָאָ֖רֶץ אֲשֶׁר־גַּ֥רְתָּה בָּֽהּ: כדוַיֹּ֙אמֶר֙ אַבְרָהָ֔ם אָנֹכִ֖י
אִשָּׁבֵֽעַ: כהוְהוֹכִ֥חַ אַבְרָהָ֖ם אֶת־אֲבִימֶ֑לֶךְ עַל־
אֹדוֹת֙ בְּאֵ֣ר הַמַּ֔יִם אֲשֶׁ֥ר גָּזְל֖וּ עַבְדֵ֥י אֲבִימֶֽלֶךְ:
כווַיֹּ֣אמֶר אֲבִימֶ֔לֶךְ לֹ֣א יָדַ֔עְתִּי מִ֥י עָשָׂ֖ה אֶת־
הַדָּבָ֣ר הַזֶּ֑ה וְגַם־אַתָּ֞ה לֹא־הִגַּ֣דְתָּ לִּ֗י וְגַ֧ם אָנֹכִ֛י
לֹ֥א שָׁמַ֖עְתִּי בִּלְתִּ֥י הַיּֽוֹם: כזוַיִּקַּ֤ח אַבְרָהָם֙ צֹ֣אן
וּבָקָ֔ר וַיִּתֵּ֖ן לַֽאֲבִימֶ֑לֶךְ וַיִּכְרְת֥וּ שְׁנֵיהֶ֖ם בְּרִֽית:
חמישי (בשבת: שביעי) כחוַיַּצֵּ֣ב אַבְרָהָ֗ם אֶת־שֶׁ֛בַע

כִּבְשֹׂ֥ת הַצֹּ֖אן לְבַדְּהֶֽן: כטוַיֹּ֥אמֶר אֲבִימֶ֖לֶךְ
אֶל־אַבְרָהָ֑ם מָ֣ה הֵ֗נָּה שֶׁ֤בַע כְּבָשֹׂת֙ הָאֵ֔לֶּה
אֲשֶׁ֥ר הִצַּ֖בְתָּ לְבַדָּֽנָה: לוַיֹּ֕אמֶר כִּ֚י אֶת־שֶׁ֣בַע
כְּבָשֹׂ֔ת תִּקַּ֖ח מִיָּדִ֑י בַּעֲבוּר֙ תִּֽהְיֶה־לִּ֣י לְעֵדָ֔ה
כִּ֥י חָפַ֖רְתִּי אֶת־הַבְּאֵ֥ר הַזֹּֽאת: לאעַל־כֵּ֗ן קָרָ֛א
לַמָּק֥וֹם הַה֖וּא בְּאֵ֣ר שָׁ֑בַע כִּ֛י שָׁ֥ם נִשְׁבְּע֖וּ
שְׁנֵיהֶֽם: לבוַיִּכְרְת֥וּ בְרִ֖ית בִּבְאֵ֣ר שָׁ֑בַע וַיָּ֣קָם
אֲבִימֶ֗לֶךְ וּפִיכֹל֙ שַׂר־צְבָא֔וֹ וַיָּשֻׁ֖בוּ אֶל־אֶ֥רֶץ
פְּלִשְׁתִּֽים: לגוַיִּטַּ֥ע אֶ֖שֶׁל בִּבְאֵ֣ר שָׁ֑בַע וַיִּקְרָא־
שָׁ֕ם בְּשֵׁ֥ם יְהֹוָ֖ה אֵ֥ל עוֹלָֽם: לדוַיָּ֧גָר אַבְרָהָ֛ם
בְּאֶ֥רֶץ פְּלִשְׁתִּ֖ים יָמִ֥ים רַבִּֽים:

King Avimelech from the land of the Philistines came to Avraham and said, "I see
that God is always with you and He always helps you. Let us make a treaty." Avraham
agreed. Then he complained that Avimelech's servants took away the well that provided
him with water. Avimelech said that he did not know about it. So the two now made an
agreement that they would be friends. They called the place Be'er Sheva.

And Avraham lived in the land of the Philistines for many years.

The following is read from the second Torah scroll: It describes the Rosh Hashanah offerings in the *Mishkan* and *Beis HaMikdash*.

במדבר כט:א-ו

אוּבַחֹ֨דֶשׁ הַשְּׁבִיעִ֜י בְּאֶחָ֣ד לַחֹ֗דֶשׁ מִֽקְרָא־
קֹ֙דֶשׁ֙ יִהְיֶ֣ה לָכֶ֔ם כָּל־מְלֶ֥אכֶת עֲבֹדָ֖ה לֹ֣א
תַעֲשׂ֑וּ י֥וֹם תְּרוּעָ֖ה יִהְיֶ֥ה לָכֶֽם: בוַעֲשִׂיתֶ֨ם
עֹלָ֜ה לְרֵ֤יחַ נִיחֹ֙חַ֙ לַֽיהֹוָ֔ה פַּ֧ר בֶּן־בָּקָ֛ר אֶחָ֖ד
אַ֣יִל אֶחָ֑ד כְּבָשִׂ֧ים בְּנֵֽי־שָׁנָ֛ה שִׁבְעָ֖ה תְּמִימִֽם:
גוּמִנְחָתָ֔ם סֹ֣לֶת בְּלוּלָ֣ה בַשֶּׁ֑מֶן שְׁלֹשָׁ֣ה

עֶשְׂרֹנִ֗ים לַפָּ֛ר שְׁנֵ֥י עֶשְׂרֹנִ֖ים לָאָֽיִל: דוְעִשָּׂר֣וֹן
אֶחָ֔ד לַכֶּ֖בֶשׂ הָאֶחָ֑ד לְשִׁבְעַ֖ת הַכְּבָשִֽׂים:
הוּשְׂעִיר־עִזִּ֥ים אֶחָ֖ד חַטָּ֑את לְכַפֵּ֖ר עֲלֵיכֶֽם:
ומִלְּבַד֩ עֹלַ֨ת הַחֹ֜דֶשׁ וּמִנְחָתָ֗הּ וְעֹלַ֤ת הַתָּמִיד֙
וּמִנְחָתָ֔הּ וְנִסְכֵּיהֶ֖ם כְּמִשְׁפָּטָ֑ם לְרֵ֣יחַ נִיחֹ֔חַ
אִשֶּׁ֖ה לַֽיהֹוָֽה:

A Closer Look

Our Sages offer a few reasons why this portion of the Torah is read on Rosh Hashanah:

1. The Torah tells us about the birth of
Yitzchak, which was decreed by Hashem on
Rosh Hashanah.

2. Hashem showed mercy and salvation to Hagar and Yishmael. We, also, beg Hashem for mercy and salvation on Rosh
Hashanah.

A Closer Look

On the first day of Rosh Hashanah we read the *Haftarah* from the
portion in *Navi* about the birth of
Shmuel HaNavi. That is because just
as Hashem remembered Sarah on Rosh
Hashanah and she then had a baby, Hashem also remembered Chanah, Shmuel's mother,
on Rosh Hashanah, and she also had a baby.

שמואל א א:א־ב:י

א וַיְהִי֩ אִ֨ישׁ אֶחָ֜ד מִן־הָרָמָתַ֛יִם צוֹפִ֖ים מֵהַ֣ר אֶפְרָ֑יִם וּשְׁמ֡וֹ אֶ֠לְקָנָ֠ה בֶּן־יְרֹחָ֧ם בֶּן־אֱלִיה֛וּא בֶּן־תֹּ֖חוּ בֶן־צ֥וּף אֶפְרָתִֽי: ב וְלוֹ֙ שְׁתֵּ֣י נָשִׁ֔ים שֵׁ֤ם אַחַת֙ חַנָּ֔ה וְשֵׁ֥ם הַשֵּׁנִ֖ית פְּנִנָּ֑ה וַיְהִ֤י לִפְנִנָּה֙ יְלָדִ֔ים וּלְחַנָּ֖ה אֵ֥ין יְלָדִֽים: ג וְעָלָה֩ הָאִ֨ישׁ הַה֤וּא מֵֽעִירוֹ֙ מִיָּמִ֣ים ׀ יָמִ֔ימָה לְהִֽשְׁתַּחֲוֺ֧ת וְלִזְבֹּ֛חַ לַיהוָ֥ה צְבָא֖וֹת בְּשִׁלֹ֑ה וְשָׁ֗ם שְׁנֵ֤י בְנֵֽי־עֵלִי֙ חָפְנִי֙ וּפִ֣נְחָ֔ס כֹּהֲנִ֖ים לַיהוָֽה: ד וַיְהִ֣י הַיּ֔וֹם וַיִּזְבַּ֖ח אֶלְקָנָ֑ה וְנָתַ֞ן לִפְנִנָּ֣ה אִשְׁתּ֗וֹ וּלְכָל־בָּנֶ֛יהָ וּבְנוֹתֶ֖יהָ מָנֽוֹת: ה וּלְחַנָּ֕ה יִתֵּ֛ן מָנָ֥ה אַחַ֖ת אַפָּ֑יִם כִּ֤י אֶת־חַנָּה֙ אָהֵ֔ב וַֽיהוָ֖ה סָגַ֥ר רַחְמָֽהּ: ו וְכִֽעֲסַ֤תָּה צָֽרָתָהּ֙ גַּם־כַּ֔עַס בַּעֲב֖וּר הַרְּעִמָ֑הּ כִּֽי־סָגַ֥ר יְהוָ֖ה בְּעַ֥ד רַחְמָֽהּ: ז וְכֵ֨ן יַעֲשֶׂ֜ה שָׁנָ֣ה בְשָׁנָ֗ה מִדֵּ֤י עֲלֹתָהּ֙ בְּבֵ֣ית יְהוָ֔ה כֵּ֖ן תַּכְעִסֶ֑נָּה וַתִּבְכֶּ֖ה וְלֹ֥א תֹאכַֽל: ח וַיֹּ֨אמֶר לָ֜הּ אֶלְקָנָ֣ה אִישָׁ֗הּ חַנָּה֙ לָ֣מֶה תִבְכִּ֔י וְלָ֙מֶה֙ לֹ֣א תֹֽאכְלִ֔י וְלָ֖מֶה יֵרַ֣ע לְבָבֵ֑ךְ הֲל֤וֹא אָֽנֹכִי֙ ט֣וֹב לָ֔ךְ מֵעֲשָׂרָ֖ה בָּנִֽים: ט וַתָּ֣קָם חַנָּ֔ה אַחֲרֵ֛י אָכְלָ֥ה בְשִׁלֹ֖ה וְאַחֲרֵ֣י שָׁתֹ֑ה וְעֵלִ֣י הַכֹּהֵ֗ן יֹשֵׁב֙ עַל־הַכִּסֵּ֔א עַל־מְזוּזַ֖ת הֵיכַ֥ל יְהוָֽה: י וְהִ֖יא מָ֣רַת נָ֑פֶשׁ וַתִּתְפַּלֵּ֥ל עַל־יְהוָ֖ה וּבָכֹ֥ה תִבְכֶּֽה: יא וַתִּדֹּ֨ר נֶ֜דֶר וַתֹּאמַ֗ר יְהוָ֤ה צְבָאוֹת֙ אִם־רָאֹ֣ה תִרְאֶ֣ה ׀ בָּעֳנִ֣י אֲמָתֶ֗ךָ וּזְכַרְתַּ֙נִי֙ וְלֹֽא־תִשְׁכַּ֣ח אֶת־אֲמָתֶ֔ךָ וְנָתַתָּ֥ה לַאֲמָתְךָ֖ זֶ֣רַע אֲנָשִׁ֑ים וּנְתַתִּ֤יו לַֽיהוָה֙ כָּל־יְמֵ֣י חַיָּ֔יו וּמוֹרָ֖ה לֹא־יַעֲלֶ֥ה עַל־רֹאשֽׁוֹ: יב וְהָיָה֙ כִּ֣י הִרְבְּתָ֔ה לְהִתְפַּלֵּ֖ל לִפְנֵ֣י יְהוָ֑ה וְעֵלִ֖י שֹׁמֵ֥ר אֶת־פִּֽיהָ: יג וְחַנָּ֗ה הִ֚יא מְדַבֶּ֣רֶת עַל־לִבָּ֔הּ רַ֚ק שְׂפָתֶ֣יהָ נָּע֔וֹת וְקוֹלָ֖הּ לֹ֣א יִשָּׁמֵ֑עַ וַיַּחְשְׁבֶ֥הָ עֵלִ֖י לְשִׁכֹּרָֽה: יד וַיֹּ֤אמֶר אֵלֶ֙יהָ֙ עֵלִ֔י עַד־מָתַ֖י תִּשְׁתַּכָּרִ֑ין הָסִ֥ירִי אֶת־יֵינֵ֖ךְ מֵעָלָֽיִךְ: טו וַתַּ֨עַן חַנָּ֤ה וַתֹּ֙אמֶר֙ לֹ֣א אֲדֹנִ֔י אִשָּׁ֤ה קְשַׁת־ר֙וּחַ֙ אָנֹ֔כִי וְיַ֥יִן וְשֵׁכָ֖ר לֹ֣א שָׁתִ֑יתִי וָאֶשְׁפֹּ֥ךְ אֶת־נַפְשִׁ֖י לִפְנֵ֥י יְהוָֽה: טז אַל־תִּתֵּן֙ אֶת־אֲמָ֣תְךָ֔ לִפְנֵ֖י בַּת־בְּלִיָּ֑עַל כִּֽי־מֵרֹ֥ב שִׂיחִ֛י וְכַעְסִ֖י דִּבַּ֥רְתִּי עַד־הֵֽנָּה: יז וַיַּ֧עַן עֵלִ֛י וַיֹּ֖אמֶר לְכִ֣י לְשָׁל֑וֹם וֵֽאלֹהֵ֣י יִשְׂרָאֵ֗ל יִתֵּן֙ אֶת־שֵׁ֣לָתֵ֔ךְ אֲשֶׁ֥ר שָׁאַ֖לְתְּ מֵעִמּֽוֹ: יח וַתֹּ֗אמֶר תִּמְצָ֧א שִׁפְחָתְךָ֛ חֵ֖ן בְּעֵינֶ֑יךָ וַתֵּ֨לֶךְ הָאִשָּׁ֤ה לְדַרְכָּהּ֙ וַתֹּאכַ֔ל וּפָנֶ֥יהָ לֹא־הָֽיוּ־לָ֖הּ עֽוֹד: יט וַיַּשְׁכִּ֣מוּ בַבֹּ֗קֶר וַיִּֽשְׁתַּחֲווּ֙ לִפְנֵ֣י יְהוָ֔ה וַיָּשֻׁ֖בוּ וַיָּבֹ֣אוּ אֶל־בֵּיתָ֑ם

הָרָמָ֔תָה וַיֵּ֤דַע אֶלְקָנָה֙ אֶת־חַנָּ֣ה אִשְׁתּ֔וֹ וַיִּזְכְּרֶ֖הָ יְהוָֽה: כ וַיְהִי֙ לִתְקֻפ֣וֹת הַיָּמִ֔ים וַתַּ֖הַר חַנָּ֑ה וַתֵּ֣לֶד בֵּ֔ן וַתִּקְרָ֤א אֶת־שְׁמוֹ֙ שְׁמוּאֵ֔ל כִּ֥י מֵיְהוָ֖ה שְׁאִלְתִּֽיו: כא וַיַּ֛עַל הָאִ֥ישׁ אֶלְקָנָ֖ה וְכָל־בֵּית֑וֹ לִזְבֹּ֧חַ לַֽיהוָ֛ה אֶת־זֶ֥בַח הַיָּמִ֖ים וְאֶת־נִדְרֽוֹ: כב וְחַנָּ֖ה לֹ֣א עָלָ֑תָה כִּֽי־אָמְרָ֣ה לְאִישָׁ֗הּ עַ֣ד יִגָּמֵ֤ל הַנַּ֙עַר֙ וַהֲבִאֹתִ֔יו וְנִרְאָה֙ אֶת־פְּנֵ֣י יְהוָ֔ה וְיָ֥שַׁב שָׁ֖ם עַד־עוֹלָֽם: כג וַיֹּ֣אמֶר לָהּ֩ אֶלְקָנָ֨ה אִישָׁ֜הּ עֲשִׂ֧י הַטּ֣וֹב בְּעֵינַ֗יִךְ שְׁבִי֙ עַד־גָּמְלֵ֣ךְ אֹת֔וֹ אַ֛ךְ יָקֵ֥ם יְהוָ֖ה אֶת־דְּבָר֑וֹ וַתֵּ֤שֶׁב הָֽאִשָּׁה֙ וַתֵּ֣ינֶק אֶת־בְּנָ֔הּ עַד־גָּמְלָ֖הּ אֹתֽוֹ: כד וַתַּעֲלֵ֨הוּ עִמָּ֜הּ כַּאֲשֶׁ֣ר גְּמָלַ֗תּוּ בְּפָרִ֤ים שְׁלֹשָׁה֙ וְאֵיפָ֨ה אַחַ֥ת קֶ֙מַח֙ וְנֵ֣בֶל יַ֔יִן וַתְּבִאֵ֥הוּ בֵית־יְהוָ֖ה שִׁל֑וֹ וְהַנַּ֖עַר נָֽעַר: כה וַֽיִּשְׁחֲט֖וּ אֶת־הַפָּ֑ר וַיָּבִ֥אוּ אֶת־הַנַּ֖עַר אֶל־עֵלִֽי: כו וַתֹּ֙אמֶר֙ בִּ֣י אֲדֹנִ֔י חֵ֥י נַפְשְׁךָ֖ אֲדֹנִ֑י אֲנִ֣י הָאִשָּׁ֗ה הַנִּצֶּ֤בֶת עִמְּכָה֙ בָּזֶ֔ה לְהִתְפַּלֵּ֖ל אֶל־יְהוָֽה: כז אֶל־הַנַּ֥עַר הַזֶּ֖ה הִתְפַּלָּ֑לְתִּי וַיִּתֵּ֨ן יְהוָ֥ה לִי֙ אֶת־שְׁאֵ֣לָתִ֔י אֲשֶׁ֥ר שָׁאַ֖לְתִּי מֵעִמּֽוֹ: כח וְגַ֣ם אָנֹכִ֗י הִשְׁאִלְתִּ֙הוּ֙ לַֽיהוָ֔ה כָּל־הַיָּמִים֙ אֲשֶׁ֣ר הָיָ֔ה ה֥וּא שָׁא֖וּל לַֽיהוָ֑ה וַיִּשְׁתַּ֥חוּ שָׁ֖ם לַֽיהוָֽה: א וַתִּתְפַּלֵּ֤ל חַנָּה֙ וַתֹּאמַ֔ר עָלַ֤ץ לִבִּי֙ בַּֽיהוָ֔ה רָ֥מָה קַרְנִ֖י בַּֽיהוָ֑ה רָ֤חַב פִּי֙ עַל־א֣וֹיְבַ֔י כִּ֥י שָׂמַ֖חְתִּי בִּישׁוּעָתֶֽךָ: ב אֵין־קָד֥וֹשׁ כַּֽיהוָ֖ה כִּ֣י אֵ֣ין בִּלְתֶּ֑ךָ וְאֵ֥ין צ֖וּר כֵּאלֹהֵֽינוּ: ג אַל־תַּרְבּ֤וּ תְדַבְּרוּ֙ גְּבֹהָ֣ה גְבֹהָ֔ה יֵצֵ֥א עָתָ֖ק מִפִּיכֶ֑ם כִּ֣י אֵ֤ל דֵּעוֹת֙ יְהוָ֔ה וְלֹ֥א [וְלוֹ כ] נִתְכְּנ֖וּ עֲלִלֽוֹת: ד קֶ֥שֶׁת גִּבֹּרִ֖ים חַתִּ֑ים וְנִכְשָׁלִ֖ים אָ֥זְרוּ חָֽיִל: ה שְׂבֵעִ֤ים בַּלֶּ֙חֶם֙ נִשְׂכָּ֔רוּ וּרְעֵבִ֖ים חָדֵ֑לּוּ עַד־עֲקָרָה֙ יָלְדָ֣ה שִׁבְעָ֔ה וְרַבַּ֥ת בָּנִ֖ים אֻמְלָֽלָה: ו יְהוָ֖ה מֵמִ֣ית וּמְחַיֶּ֑ה מוֹרִ֥יד שְׁא֖וֹל וַיָּֽעַל: ז יְהוָ֖ה מוֹרִ֣ישׁ וּמַעֲשִׁ֑יר מַשְׁפִּ֖יל אַף־מְרוֹמֵֽם: ח מֵקִ֨ים מֵעָפָ֜ר דָּ֗ל מֵֽאַשְׁפֹּת֙ יָרִ֣ים אֶבְי֔וֹן לְהוֹשִׁיב֙ עִם־נְדִיבִ֔ים וְכִסֵּ֥א כָב֖וֹד יַנְחִלֵ֑ם כִּ֤י לַֽיהוָה֙ מְצֻ֣קֵי אֶ֔רֶץ וַיָּ֥שֶׁת עֲלֵיהֶ֖ם תֵּבֵֽל: ט רַגְלֵ֤י חֲסִידָיו֙ [חֲסִידוֹ כ] יִשְׁמֹ֔ר וּרְשָׁעִ֖ים בַּחֹ֣שֶׁךְ יִדָּ֑מּוּ כִּֽי־לֹ֥א בְכֹ֖חַ יִגְבַּר־אִֽישׁ: י יְהוָ֞ה יֵחַ֣תּוּ מְרִיבָ֗יו [מְרִיבוֹ כ] עָלָיו֙ [עָלוֹ כ] בַּשָּׁמַ֣יִם יַרְעֵ֔ם יְהוָ֖ה יָדִ֣ין אַפְסֵי־אָ֑רֶץ וְיִתֶּן־עֹ֣ז לְמַלְכּ֔וֹ וְיָרֵ֖ם קֶ֥רֶן מְשִׁיחֽוֹ:

קְרִיאַת הַתּוֹרָה - יוֹם שֵׁנִי / *Torah Reading – Second Day*

On the second day, we read about the story of the Binding of Yitzchak, also found in *Chumash Bereishis*.

The English beneath the Hebrew text is a concise adaptation of the story.

בראשית פרק כב

כהן - אוַיְהִי אַחַר הַדְּבָרִים הָאֵלֶּה וְהָאֱלֹהִים נִסָּה אֶת־אַבְרָהָם וַיֹּאמֶר אֵלָיו אַבְרָהָם וַיֹּאמֶר הִנֵּנִי: בוַיֹּאמֶר קַח־נָא אֶת־בִּנְךָ אֶת־יְחִידְךָ אֲשֶׁר־אָהַבְתָּ אֶת־יִצְחָק וְלֶךְ־לְךָ אֶל־אֶרֶץ הַמֹּרִיָּה וְהַעֲלֵהוּ שָׁם לְעֹלָה עַל אַחַד הֶהָרִים אֲשֶׁר אֹמַר אֵלֶיךָ: גוַיַּשְׁכֵּם אַבְרָהָם בַּבֹּקֶר וַיַּחֲבֹשׁ אֶת־חֲמֹרוֹ וַיִּקַּח אֶת־שְׁנֵי נְעָרָיו אִתּוֹ וְאֵת יִצְחָק בְּנוֹ וַיְבַקַּע עֲצֵי עֹלָה וַיָּקָם וַיֵּלֶךְ אֶל־הַמָּקוֹם אֲשֶׁר־אָמַר־לוֹ הָאֱלֹהִים:

לוי - דבַּיּוֹם הַשְּׁלִישִׁי וַיִּשָּׂא אַבְרָהָם אֶת־עֵינָיו וַיַּרְא אֶת־הַמָּקוֹם מֵרָחֹק: הוַיֹּאמֶר אַבְרָהָם אֶל־נְעָרָיו שְׁבוּ־לָכֶם פֹּה עִם־הַחֲמוֹר וַאֲנִי וְהַנַּעַר נֵלְכָה עַד־כֹּה וְנִשְׁתַּחֲוֶה וְנָשׁוּבָה אֲלֵיכֶם: ווַיִּקַּח אַבְרָהָם אֶת־עֲצֵי הָעֹלָה וַיָּשֶׂם עַל־יִצְחָק בְּנוֹ וַיִּקַּח בְּיָדוֹ אֶת־הָאֵשׁ וְאֶת־הַמַּאֲכֶלֶת וַיֵּלְכוּ שְׁנֵיהֶם יַחְדָּו: זוַיֹּאמֶר יִצְחָק אֶל־אַבְרָהָם אָבִיו וַיֹּאמֶר אָבִי וַיֹּאמֶר הִנֶּנִּי בְנִי וַיֹּאמֶר הִנֵּה הָאֵשׁ וְהָעֵצִים וְאַיֵּה הַשֶּׂה לְעֹלָה: חוַיֹּאמֶר אַבְרָהָם אֱלֹהִים יִרְאֶה־לּוֹ הַשֶּׂה לְעֹלָה בְּנִי וַיֵּלְכוּ שְׁנֵיהֶם יַחְדָּו:

שלישי - טוַיָּבֹאוּ אֶל־הַמָּקוֹם אֲשֶׁר אָמַר־לוֹ הָאֱלֹהִים וַיִּבֶן שָׁם אַבְרָהָם אֶת־הַמִּזְבֵּחַ וַיַּעֲרֹךְ אֶת־הָעֵצִים וַיַּעֲקֹד אֶת־יִצְחָק בְּנוֹ וַיָּשֶׂם אֹתוֹ עַל־הַמִּזְבֵּחַ מִמַּעַל לָעֵצִים: יוַיִּשְׁלַח אַבְרָהָם אֶת־יָדוֹ וַיִּקַּח אֶת־הַמַּאֲכֶלֶת לִשְׁחֹט אֶת־בְּנוֹ: יאוַיִּקְרָא אֵלָיו מַלְאַךְ יהוה מִן־הַשָּׁמַיִם וַיֹּאמֶר אַבְרָהָם | אַבְרָהָם וַיֹּאמֶר הִנֵּנִי: יבוַיֹּאמֶר אַל־תִּשְׁלַח יָדְךָ אֶל־הַנַּעַר וְאַל־תַּעַשׂ לוֹ מְאוּמָה כִּי | עַתָּה יָדַעְתִּי כִּי־יְרֵא אֱלֹהִים אַתָּה וְלֹא חָשַׂכְתָּ אֶת־בִּנְךָ אֶת־יְחִידְךָ מִמֶּנִּי: יגוַיִּשָּׂא אַבְרָהָם אֶת־עֵינָיו וַיַּרְא וְהִנֵּה־אַיִל אַחַר נֶאֱחַז בַּסְּבַךְ בְּקַרְנָיו וַיֵּלֶךְ אַבְרָהָם וַיִּקַּח אֶת־הָאַיִל וַיַּעֲלֵהוּ לְעֹלָה תַּחַת בְּנוֹ: ידוַיִּקְרָא אַבְרָהָם שֵׁם־הַמָּקוֹם הַהוּא יהוה | יִרְאֶה אֲשֶׁר יֵאָמֵר הַיּוֹם בְּהַר יהוה יֵרָאֶה:

רביעי - טווַיִּקְרָא מַלְאַךְ יהוה אֶל־אַבְרָהָם שֵׁנִית מִן־הַשָּׁמָיִם: טזוַיֹּאמֶר בִּי נִשְׁבַּעְתִּי נְאֻם־יהוה כִּי יַעַן אֲשֶׁר עָשִׂיתָ אֶת־הַדָּבָר הַזֶּה וְלֹא חָשַׂכְתָּ אֶת־בִּנְךָ אֶת־יְחִידֶךָ: יזכִּי־בָרֵךְ אֲבָרֶכְךָ וְהַרְבָּה אַרְבֶּה אֶת־זַרְעֲךָ כְּכוֹכְבֵי הַשָּׁמַיִם וְכַחוֹל אֲשֶׁר עַל־שְׂפַת הַיָּם וְיִרַשׁ זַרְעֲךָ אֵת שַׁעַר אֹיְבָיו:

After Yitzchak grew up, Hashem tested Avraham. "Please take your only son, your beloved son, Yitzchak," Hashem commanded, "and go to the Land of Moriah. Bring him to the mountain there and bring him as an offering to Me on an altar."

The next day, Avraham woke up early in the morning. He called his son and they went together to Har Hamoriah. Avraham brought wood and other tools, and also brought Yishmael and Eliezer along to help.

On the third day, Avraham saw the mountain. "You two stay here," Avraham told the helpers. "Yitzchak and I will go up to the mountain."

Our Sages teach us that when Avraham sacrificed the ram on Har Hamoriah instead of his son Yitzchak, the two horns were put away for future use. The left horn was the shofar sounded when the Torah was given at Har Sinai, and the right horn will be blown one day to announce the arrival of *Mashiach*.

וְהִתְבָּרֲכ֣וּ בְזַרְעֲךָ֔ כֹּ֖ל גּוֹיֵ֣י הָאָ֑רֶץ עֵ֕קֶב אֲשֶׁ֥ר שָׁמַ֖עְתָּ בְּקֹלִֽי: יטוַיָּ֤שָׁב אַבְרָהָם֙ אֶל־נְעָרָ֔יו וַיָּקֻ֛מוּ וַיֵּלְכ֥וּ יַחְדָּ֖ו אֶל־בְּאֵ֣ר שָׁ֑בַע וַיֵּ֥שֶׁב אַבְרָהָ֖ם בִּבְאֵ֥ר שָֽׁבַע:

חמישי - כוַיְהִ֗י אַחֲרֵי֙ הַדְּבָרִ֣ים הָאֵ֔לֶּה וַיֻּגַּ֥ד לְאַבְרָהָ֖ם לֵאמֹ֑ר הִ֠נֵּה יָלְדָ֨ה מִלְכָּ֥ה גַם־הִ֛וא בָּנִ֖ים לְנָח֥וֹר

אָחִֽיךָ: כאאֶת־ע֥וּץ בְּכֹר֖וֹ וְאֶת־בּ֣וּז אָחִ֑יו וְאֶת־קְמוּאֵ֖ל אֲבִ֥י אֲרָֽם: כבוְאֶת־כֶּ֣שֶׂד וְאֶת־חֲז֔וֹ וְאֶת־פִּלְדָּ֖שׁ וְאֶת־יִדְלָ֑ף וְאֵ֖ת בְּתוּאֵֽל: כגוּבְתוּאֵ֖ל יָלַ֣ד אֶת־רִבְקָ֑ה שְׁמֹנָ֥ה אֵ֙לֶּה֙ יָלְדָ֣ה מִלְכָּ֔ה לְנָח֖וֹר אֲחִ֥י אַבְרָהָֽם: כדוּפִֽילַגְשׁ֖וֹ וּשְׁמָ֣הּ רְאוּמָ֑ה וַתֵּ֤לֶד גַּם־הִוא֙ אֶת־טֶ֣בַח וְאֶת־גַּ֔חַם וְאֶת־תַּ֖חַשׁ וְאֶת־מַעֲכָֽה:

Avraham took wood, fire, and his knife and went with Yitzchak. "But, Father," Yitzchak asked, "I see the fire and the wood, but where is the lamb for the offering?"

"Don't worry," answered Avraham. "Hashem will show the offering, my son." And together, the two climbed Har Hamoriah.

Avraham built an altar and placed wood on top of it. Avraham tied Yitzchak onto the altar. Stretching his hand, Avraham grabbed the knife.

Suddenly, an angel of Hashem called to him, "Avraham, Avraham, Hashem has sent me to tell you that you should not hurt your son." Avraham untied Yitzchak. He saw a ram caught in the bushes and sacrificed it instead of his son.

Then Hashem made a promise to Avraham. "Because you listened to Me, I will bless you and make you into a great nation."

Avraham and Yitzchak returned home to Be'er Sheva.

The following is read from the second Torah scroll: It describes the Rosh Hashanah offerings in the *Mishkan* and *Beis HaMikdash*.

במדבר כט:א־ו

אוּבַחֹ֨דֶשׁ הַשְּׁבִיעִ֜י בְּאֶחָ֣ד לַחֹ֗דֶשׁ מִֽקְרָא־קֹ֙דֶשׁ֙ יִהְיֶ֣ה לָכֶ֔ם כָּל־מְלֶ֥אכֶת עֲבֹדָ֖ה לֹ֣א תַעֲשׂ֑וּ י֥וֹם תְּרוּעָ֖ה יִהְיֶ֥ה לָכֶֽם: בוַעֲשִׂיתֶ֨ם עֹלָ֜ה לְרֵ֤יחַ נִיחֹ֙חַ֙ לַֽיהֹוָ֔ה פַּ֧ר בֶּן־בָּקָ֛ר אֶחָ֖ד אַ֣יִל אֶחָ֑ד כְּבָשִׂ֧ים בְּנֵֽי־שָׁנָ֛ה שִׁבְעָ֖ה תְּמִימִֽם: גוּמִ֨נְחָתָ֔ם סֹ֖לֶת בְּלוּלָ֣ה

בַשָּׁ֑מֶן שְׁלֹשָׁ֤ה עֶשְׂרֹנִים֙ לַפָּ֔ר שְׁנֵ֥י עֶשְׂרֹנִ֖ים לָאָֽיִל: דוְעִשָּׂר֣וֹן אֶחָ֔ד לַכֶּ֖בֶשׂ הָאֶחָ֑ד לְשִׁבְעַ֖ת הַכְּבָשִֽׂים: הוּשְׂעִיר־עִזִּ֥ים אֶחָ֖ד חַטָּ֑את לְכַפֵּ֖ר עֲלֵיכֶֽם: מִלְּבַ֞ד עֹלַ֤ת הַחֹ֙דֶשׁ֙ וּמִנְחָתָ֔הּ וְעֹלַ֥ת הַתָּמִ֖יד וּמִנְחָתָ֑הּ וְנִסְכֵּיהֶ֛ם כְּמִשְׁפָּטָ֖ם לְרֵ֣יחַ נִיחֹ֔חַ אִשֶּׁ֖ה לַיהֹוָֽה:

A Closer Look

We always mention our three *Avos* (forefathers) when we ask for mercy and forgiveness. After the Jewish people sinned in the desert, Moshe said, "Remember Your servants, Avraham, Yitzchak, and Yaakov." And Hashem forgave His people for their sake.

A Closer Look

We read this section of the Torah now because the story of the Binding of Yitzchak happened on Rosh Hashanah. Also, the shofar is made of a ram's horn to remind us and Hashem how Avraham was willing to sacrifice his son for Him. The ram was substituted for Yitzchak on the altar.

ירמיה לא:א–יט

כֹּה אָמַר יהוֹה מָצָא חֵן בַּמִּדְבָּר עַם שְׂרִידֵי חָרֶב הָלוֹךְ לְהַרְגִּיעוֹ יִשְׂרָאֵל: מֵרָחוֹק יהוה נִרְאָה לִי וְאַהֲבַת עוֹלָם אֲהַבְתִּיךְ עַל־כֵּן מְשַׁכְתִּיךְ חָסֶד: עוֹד אֶבְנֵךְ וְנִבְנֵית בְּתוּלַת יִשְׂרָאֵל עוֹד תַּעְדִּי תֻפַּיִךְ וְיָצָאת בִּמְחוֹל מְשַׂחֲקִים: עוֹד תִּטְּעִי כְרָמִים בְּהָרֵי שֹׁמְרוֹן נָטְעוּ נֹטְעִים וְחִלֵּלוּ: כִּי יֶשׁ־יוֹם קָרְאוּ נֹצְרִים בְּהַר אֶפְרָיִם קוּמוּ וְנַעֲלֶה צִיּוֹן אֶל־יהוה אֱלֹהֵינוּ: כִּי־כֹה | אָמַר יהוה רָנּוּ לְיַעֲקֹב שִׂמְחָה וְצַהֲלוּ בְּרֹאשׁ הַגּוֹיִם הַשְׁמִיעוּ הַלְלוּ וְאִמְרוּ הוֹשַׁע יהוה אֶת־עַמְּךָ אֵת שְׁאֵרִית יִשְׂרָאֵל: הִנְנִי מֵבִיא אוֹתָם מֵאֶרֶץ צָפוֹן וְקִבַּצְתִּים מִיַּרְכְּתֵי־אָרֶץ בָּם עִוֵּר וּפִסֵּחַ הָרָה וְיֹלֶדֶת יַחְדָּו קָהָל גָּדוֹל יָשׁוּבוּ הֵנָּה: בִּבְכִי יָבֹאוּ וּבְתַחֲנוּנִים אוֹבִילֵם אוֹלִיכֵם אֶל־נַחֲלֵי מַיִם בְּדֶרֶךְ יָשָׁר לֹא יִכָּשְׁלוּ בָּהּ כִּי־הָיִיתִי לְיִשְׂרָאֵל לְאָב וְאֶפְרַיִם בְּכֹרִי הוּא: שִׁמְעוּ דְבַר־יהוה גּוֹיִם וְהַגִּידוּ בָאִיִּים מִמֶּרְחָק וְאִמְרוּ מְזָרֵה יִשְׂרָאֵל יְקַבְּצֶנּוּ וּשְׁמָרוֹ כְּרֹעֶה עֶדְרוֹ: כִּי־פָדָה יהוה אֶת־יַעֲקֹב וּגְאָלוֹ מִיַּד חָזָק מִמֶּנּוּ: וּבָאוּ וְרִנְּנוּ בִמְרוֹם־צִיּוֹן

וְנָהֲרוּ אֶל־טוּב יהוה עַל־דָּגָן וְעַל־תִּירֹשׁ וְעַל־יִצְהָר וְעַל־בְּנֵי־צֹאן וּבָקָר וְהָיְתָה נַפְשָׁם כְּגַן רָוֶה וְלֹא־יוֹסִיפוּ לְדַאֲבָה עוֹד: אָז תִּשְׂמַח בְּתוּלָה בְּמָחוֹל וּבַחֻרִים וּזְקֵנִים יַחְדָּו וְהָפַכְתִּי אֶבְלָם לְשָׂשׂוֹן וְנִחַמְתִּים וְשִׂמַּחְתִּים מִיגוֹנָם: וְרִוֵּיתִי נֶפֶשׁ הַכֹּהֲנִים דֶּשֶׁן וְעַמִּי אֶת־טוּבִי יִשְׂבָּעוּ נְאֻם־יהוה: כֹּה | אָמַר יהוה קוֹל בְּרָמָה נִשְׁמָע נְהִי בְּכִי תַמְרוּרִים רָחֵל מְבַכָּה עַל־בָּנֶיהָ מֵאֲנָה לְהִנָּחֵם עַל־בָּנֶיהָ כִּי אֵינֶנּוּ: כֹּה | אָמַר יהוה מִנְעִי קוֹלֵךְ מִבֶּכִי וְעֵינַיִךְ מִדִּמְעָה כִּי יֵשׁ שָׂכָר לִפְעֻלָּתֵךְ נְאֻם־יהוה וְשָׁבוּ מֵאֶרֶץ אוֹיֵב: וְיֵשׁ־תִּקְוָה לְאַחֲרִיתֵךְ נְאֻם־יהוה וְשָׁבוּ בָנִים לִגְבוּלָם: שָׁמוֹעַ שָׁמַעְתִּי אֶפְרַיִם מִתְנוֹדֵד יִסַּרְתַּנִי וָאִוָּסֵר כְּעֵגֶל לֹא לֻמָּד הֲשִׁיבֵנִי וְאָשׁוּבָה כִּי אַתָּה יהוה אֱלֹהָי: כִּי־אַחֲרֵי שׁוּבִי נִחַמְתִּי וְאַחֲרֵי הִוָּדְעִי סָפַקְתִּי עַל־יָרֵךְ בֹּשְׁתִּי וְגַם־נִכְלַמְתִּי כִּי נָשָׂאתִי חֶרְפַּת נְעוּרָי: הֲבֵן יַקִּיר לִי אֶפְרַיִם אִם יֶלֶד שַׁעֲשֻׁעִים כִּי־מִדֵּי דַבְּרִי בּוֹ זָכֹר אֶזְכְּרֶנּוּ עוֹד עַל־כֵּן הָמוּ מֵעַי לוֹ רַחֵם אֲרַחֲמֶנּוּ נְאֻם־יהוה:

A Closer Look

This *Haftarah* gives us a beautiful picture of how wonderful it will be when *Mashiach* comes.

Did You Know??

The last verse of this *Haftarah* also appears in the *Zichronos* section of *Mussaf* (see page 46).

תְּקִיעַת שׁוֹפָר / Shofar Blowing

At the end of time, all the nations of the world will join forces to fight against Hashem and the Jewish People, but they will be defeated. This psalm talks about what the world will be like after the nations lose the battle and recognize that Hashem is the true Ruler of the world.

This psalm also shows us how the sound of the shofar inspires and arouses Hashem's mercy.

For the Conductor of the music. A Psalm by the sons of Korach. All the nations of the world should join their hands together. They should call out to Hashem with joy. Because Hashem is the Most High. He is a great King, ruling over the entire world. He will lead the nations to be under our rule. He will choose our portion for us (Eretz Yisrael), the pride of Yaakov (the *Beis HaMikdash*), which He loves, *Selah*. Hashem rises up high (becoming praised) with the shofar blast (in the *Beis HaMikdash*). Sing praises to Hashem, sing praises. Sing praises to our King, sing praises. Because Hashem is the King of the entire world. Sing a song to Him, you who are wise. Hashem is King over all the nations of the world. He sits on His holy throne. The important people of all the nations joined together, the people who worship the God of Avraham. Hashem controls the rulers of the world. He is very exalted!

לַמְנַצֵּחַ לִבְנֵי קֹרַח מִזְמוֹר. כָּל הָעַמִּים תִּקְעוּ כָף, הָרִיעוּ לֵאלֹהִים בְּקוֹל רִנָּה. כִּי יהוה עֶלְיוֹן נוֹרָא, מֶלֶךְ גָּדוֹל עַל כָּל הָאָרֶץ. יַדְבֵּר עַמִּים תַּחְתֵּינוּ, וּלְאֻמִּים תַּחַת רַגְלֵינוּ. יִבְחַר לָנוּ אֶת נַחֲלָתֵנוּ, אֶת גְּאוֹן יַעֲקֹב אֲשֶׁר אָהֵב סֶלָה. עָלָה אֱלֹהִים בִּתְרוּעָה, יהוה בְּקוֹל שׁוֹפָר. זַמְּרוּ אֱלֹהִים זַמֵּרוּ, זַמְּרוּ לְמַלְכֵּנוּ זַמֵּרוּ. כִּי מֶלֶךְ כָּל הָאָרֶץ אֱלֹהִים, זַמְּרוּ מַשְׂכִּיל. מָלַךְ אֱלֹהִים עַל גּוֹיִם, אֱלֹהִים יָשַׁב עַל כִּסֵּא קָדְשׁוֹ. נְדִיבֵי עַמִּים נֶאֱסָפוּ עַם אֱלֹהֵי אַבְרָהָם, כִּי לֵאלֹהִים מָגִנֵּי אֶרֶץ, מְאֹד נַעֲלָה.

Did You Know??
Our Rabbis disagree as to which period of Jewish history this psalm is referring. Some say it refers to the future — to the time of *Mashiach*. Some say it refers to the time when the Jews suffered under the rule of King Nebuchadnezzar during the Babylonian exile. And some say it is referring to the time when David HaMelech was bringing the Holy Ark to its home in Yerushalayim for the first time.

A Closer Look
This psalm was written by the sons of Korach. But it was later changed by David HaMelech, so that it would be appreciated by all future generations.

The chazzan says each verse, and everyone repeats after him.

From my troubles I called to Hashem and He answered me generously.	מִן הַמֵּצַר קָרָאתִי יָּה, עָנָנִי בַמֶּרְחָב יָּה.
You have heard my voice, do not close Your ear from my prayers.	קוֹלִי שָׁמָעְתָּ, אַל תַּעְלֵם אָזְנְךָ לְרַוְחָתִי לְשַׁוְעָתִי.
Your very first words are truth, and Your fair judgment is forever.	רֹאשׁ דְּבָרְךָ אֱמֶת, וּלְעוֹלָם כָּל מִשְׁפַּט צִדְקֶךָ.
Guarantee only good for Your servants, and do not let sinners take advantage of me.	עֲרֹב עַבְדְּךָ לְטוֹב, אַל יַעַשְׁקֻנִי זֵדִים.
I am joyous about everything You say, like someone who finds a treasure.	שָׂשׂ אָנֹכִי עַל אִמְרָתֶךָ, כְּמוֹצֵא שָׁלָל רָב.
Teach me to be wise, because I believe in Your commandments.	טוּב טַעַם וָדַעַת לַמְּדֵנִי, כִּי בְמִצְוֹתֶיךָ הֶאֱמָנְתִּי.
Accept the words that I say, Hashem, and teach me Your laws.	נִדְבוֹת פִּי רְצֵה נָא, יהוה, וּמִשְׁפָּטֶיךָ לַמְּדֵנִי.

The "baal tokei'ah," the person who blows the shofar, says these blessings aloud. Everyone listens carefully and answers Amen to each one. From here until the end of the shofar blasts we may not speak until we are finished with the davening.

Blessed are You, Hashem, our God, King of the universe, Who has made us holy with His mitzvos, and commanded us to hear the sound of the shofar.	בָּרוּךְ אַתָּה יהוה אֱלֹהֵינוּ מֶלֶךְ הָעוֹלָם, אֲשֶׁר קִדְּשָׁנוּ בְּמִצְוֹתָיו, וְצִוָּנוּ לִשְׁמוֹעַ קוֹל שׁוֹפָר.
Blessed are You, Hashem, our God, King of the universe, for keeping us alive, taking care of us, and bringing us to this time.	בָּרוּךְ אַתָּה יהוה אֱלֹהֵינוּ מֶלֶךְ הָעוֹלָם, שֶׁהֶחֱיָנוּ וְקִיְּמָנוּ וְהִגִּיעָנוּ לַזְּמַן הַזֶּה.

The makrei calls out the names of the sounds for the baal tokei'ah to blow.

Tekiah Shevarim-Teruah Tekiah	תְּקִיעָה. שְׁבָרִים־תְּרוּעָה. תְּקִיעָה.
Tekiah Shevarim-Teruah Tekiah	תְּקִיעָה. שְׁבָרִים־תְּרוּעָה. תְּקִיעָה.
Tekiah Shevarim-Teruah Tekiah	תְּקִיעָה. שְׁבָרִים־תְּרוּעָה. תְּקִיעָה.
Tekiah Shevarim Tekiah	תְּקִיעָה. שְׁבָרִים. תְּקִיעָה.
Tekiah Shevarim Tekiah	תְּקִיעָה. שְׁבָרִים. תְּקִיעָה.
Tekiah Shevarim Tekiah	תְּקִיעָה. שְׁבָרִים. תְּקִיעָה.

We blow the shofar at different times during Mussaf. Each time, the last sound of the shofar is a Tekiah Gedolah (an extra-long tekiah blast).

Tekiah Teruah Tekiah	תְּקִיעָה. תְּרוּעָה. תְּקִיעָה.
Tekiah Teruah Tekiah	תְּקִיעָה. תְּרוּעָה. תְּקִיעָה.
Tekiah Teruah Tekiah	תְּקִיעָה. תְּרוּעָה. תְּקִיעָה־גְדוֹלָה.

(For more about shofar and shofar-blowing, see page 8.)

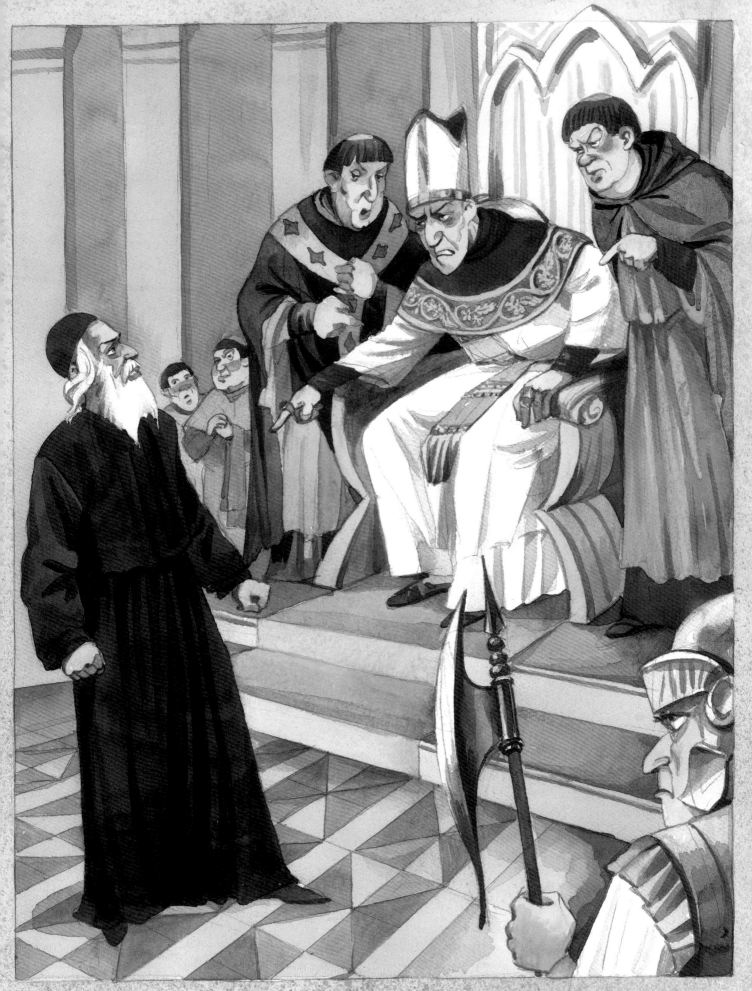

וּנְתַנֶּה תֹּקֶף / Unesaneh Tokef

Let us now describe how holy this day is. This day is fearful and frightening. On this day Your kingship will be exalted, Your throne will be based on kindness, and You will sit upon it in truth. It is You alone Who judges and proves, knows and testifies; it is You Who writes and seals our fate. You remember everything that was forgotten. You will open the Book of Memories, and the Book will call out what everyone has done during the year and each person's signature is there, (saying that it is true). A great shofar will be sounded, but only a quiet, frail noise is heard. Angels will rush, tremble and be afraid. They will say, "Behold, it is the Day of Judgment — to judge the host of Heaven." For even angels are not perfect if they would be judged strictly. Everyone will pass before You, one at a time, like sheep in a flock.

You are like a shepherd inspecting his flock of sheep, making his sheep pass under his stick. You, too, make every person pass in front of You to be counted and judged. You will decide each person's fate, and write their verdict.

וּנְתַנֶּה תֹּקֶף קְדֻשַּׁת הַיּוֹם, כִּי הוּא נוֹרָא וְאָיֹם. וּבוֹ תִנָּשֵׂא מַלְכוּתֶךָ, וְיִכּוֹן בְּחֶסֶד כִּסְאֶךָ, וְתֵשֵׁב עָלָיו בֶּאֱמֶת. אֱמֶת כִּי אַתָּה הוּא דַיָּן וּמוֹכִיחַ, וְיוֹדֵעַ וָעֵד, וְכוֹתֵב וְחוֹתֵם (וְסוֹפֵר וּמוֹנֶה), וְתִזְכֹּר כָּל הַנִּשְׁכָּחוֹת. וְתִפְתַּח אֶת סֵפֶר הַזִּכְרוֹנוֹת, וּמֵאֵלָיו יִקָּרֵא, וְחוֹתָם יַד כָּל אָדָם בּוֹ. וּבְשׁוֹפָר גָּדוֹל יִתָּקַע, וְקוֹל דְּמָמָה דַקָּה יִשָּׁמַע. וּמַלְאָכִים יֵחָפֵזוּן, וְחִיל וּרְעָדָה יֹאחֵזוּן, וְיֹאמְרוּ הִנֵּה יוֹם הַדִּין, לִפְקֹד עַל צְבָא מָרוֹם בַּדִּין, כִּי לֹא יִזְכּוּ בְעֵינֶיךָ בַּדִּין. וְכָל בָּאֵי עוֹלָם יַעַבְרוּן לְפָנֶיךָ כִּבְנֵי מָרוֹן. כְּבַקָּרַת רוֹעֶה עֶדְרוֹ, מַעֲבִיר צֹאנוֹ תַּחַת שִׁבְטוֹ, כֵּן תַּעֲבִיר וְתִסְפֹּר וְתִמְנֶה, וְתִפְקֹד נֶפֶשׁ כָּל חָי, וְתַחְתֹּךְ קִצְבָה לְכָל בְּרִיּוֹתֶיךָ, וְתִכְתֹּב אֶת גְּזַר דִּינָם.

A Closer Look
   Unesaneh Tokef is considered one of the most holy and moving prayers said on Rosh Hashanah and Yom Kippur. It tells us how Hashem is judging each of us, one at a time. Even though the world is filled with millions of people, everyone is judged separately, as a unique individual. Whatever happens to each person was decided by Hashem

Did You Know??
   This prayer was written by R' Amnon of Mainz in Germany about 1,000 years ago. One day, the Bishop of Mainz demanded that his friend and adviser, R' Amnon, become a Christian. R' Amnon became frightened and asked for three days to think it over. When he got home he felt very bad. *Why did I tell the bishop that I need three days to think about this?* he thought. *I should have said no, immediately!* R' Amnon fasted and repented and did not return to the bishop.
   After three days, the bishop had R' Amnon brought to his castle. "Why did you not come here after three days?" the bishop shouted. He was very angry.
   R' Amnon replied, "I should have immediately said no. May my tongue be cut out for pretending I would even think about your request."
   "No," the bishop screamed, "it was your legs that sinned, by not coming back here in three days." The bishop's servants then cut off R' Amnon's legs and also cut off his hands as a further punishment.
   Afterward, R' Amnon was brought home, bleeding and dying. A few days later, Rosh Hashanah arrived. R' Amnon asked to be brought to his shul. In front of the *Aron Kodesh*, he recited this prayer — *Unesaneh Tokef*. Upon finishing the prayer, he died.

בְּרֹאשׁ הַשָּׁנָה יִכָּתֵבוּן, וּבְיוֹם צוֹם כִּפּוּר יֵחָתֵמוּן, כַּמָּה יַעַבְרוּן, וְכַמָּה יִבָּרֵאוּן; מִי יִחְיֶה וּמִי יָמוּת, מִי בְקִצּוֹ וּמִי לֹא בְקִצּוֹ; מִי בַמַּיִם וּמִי בָאֵשׁ, מִי בַחֶרֶב וּמִי בַחַיָּה, מִי בָרָעָב וּמִי בַצָּמָא, מִי בָרַעַשׁ וּמִי בַמַּגֵּפָה, מִי בַחֲנִיקָה וּמִי בַסְּקִילָה; מִי יָנוּחַ וּמִי יָנוּעַ, מִי יִשָּׁקֵט וּמִי יִטָּרֵף, מִי יִשָּׁלֵו וּמִי יִתְיַסָּר, מִי יֵעָנִי וּמִי יֵעָשֵׁר, מִי יִשָּׁפֵל וּמִי יָרוּם.

On Rosh Hashanah our fate is written, and on Yom Kippur it is sealed. How many will die and how many will be born; who will live and who will die; who will die at his proper time, and who will die before his time; who will die by water, and who by fire; who by sword, and who by an animal; who by hunger, and who by thirst; who by a storm, and who by a plague; who by choking and who by stoning; who will rest comfortably, and who will wander from place to place; who will live quietly and who will be pressured; who will live peacefully and who will suffer; who will be poor, and who will be rich; who will be brought down, and who will be uplifted.

A Closer Look

This prayer shows us that everything happens only because it is decreed by Hashem. Even if something looks like an accident, it really happened because Hashem said it should. Everyone's successes and everyone's failures are decreed by Hashem. And it is on Rosh Hashanah and Yom Kippur that He judges and decrees what kind of year we will have.

A Closer Look

In order to do *teshuvah*, first a person must be sorry for what he did, then he must decide never to do it again, then he must ask Hashem to forgive him. If possible, the person should try to correct whatever wrong was done. If the person has harmed someone else, Hashem will not forgive until he apologizes to the person and the person forgives him.

וּתְשׁוּבָה וּתְפִלָּה וּצְדָקָה
מַעֲבִירִין אֶת רֹעַ הַגְּזֵרָה.

But *Teshuvah* (repentance), *Tefillah* (prayer), and *Tzedakah* (charity) change an evil decree.

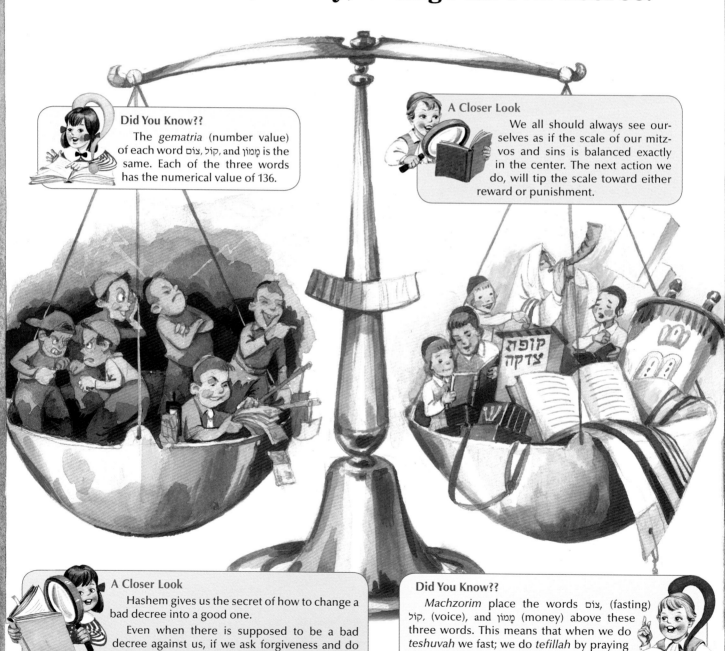

Did You Know??

The *gematria* (number value) of each word צוֹם, קוֹל, and מָמוֹן is the same. Each of the three words has the numerical value of 136.

A Closer Look

We all should always see ourselves as if the scale of our mitzvos and sins is balanced exactly in the center. The next action we do, will tip the scale toward either reward or punishment.

A Closer Look

Hashem gives us the secret of how to change a bad decree into a good one.

Even when there is supposed to be a bad decree against us, if we ask forgiveness and do *teshuvah*, pray to Hashem, and give charity, that bad decree can be changed to a good decree.

Did You Know??

Machzorim place the words צוֹם, (fasting) קוֹל, (voice), and מָמוֹן (money) above these three words. This means that when we do *teshuvah* we fast; we do *tefillah* by praying in a loud voice, and we do *tzedakah* by giving money.

Your Name (of mercy) shows Your praise. You do not get angry easily, and You forgive easily. You do not wish for someone to die, even if he deserves it; for You hope that he will repent and live. In fact, You wait for him to repent until the day he dies. If he repents, You will forgive him right away.

It is true that You created everyone, and You know what they are thinking, because they are only made of flesh and blood. Man comes from dust, and to dust he will return. He risks his life every day just to earn some bread to eat. Man is like a broken piece of pottery, a dying blade of grass, a fading flower, a passing shadow, a dissapearing cloud, a blowing wind, dust flying in the air, and a dream that is gone when the person wakes up.

כִּי כְּשִׁמְךָ כֵּן תְּהִלָּתֶךָ, קָשֶׁה לִכְעֹס וְנוֹחַ לִרְצוֹת; כִּי לֹא תַחְפֹּץ בְּמוֹת הַמֵּת, כִּי אִם בְּשׁוּבוֹ מִדַּרְכּוֹ וְחָיָה. וְעַד יוֹם מוֹתוֹ תְּחַכֶּה לּוֹ, אִם יָשׁוּב מִיַּד תְּקַבְּלוֹ.

אֱמֶת כִּי אַתָּה הוּא יוֹצְרָם, וְאַתָּה יוֹדֵעַ יִצְרָם, כִּי הֵם בָּשָׂר וָדָם. אָדָם יְסוֹדוֹ מֵעָפָר וְסוֹפוֹ לֶעָפָר; בְּנַפְשׁוֹ יָבִיא לַחְמוֹ; מָשׁוּל כְּחֶרֶס הַנִּשְׁבָּר, כְּחָצִיר יָבֵשׁ וּכְצִיץ נוֹבֵל, וּכְצֵל עוֹבֵר וּכְעָנָן כָּלָה, וּכְרוּחַ נוֹשָׁבֶת, וּכְאָבָק פּוֹרֵחַ, וְכַחֲלוֹם יָעוּף.

A Closer Look
The Name that is being constantly referred to here is the Four-Letter Name י-ה-ו-ה. This is the Name of Hashem that shows His willingness to be merciful and to forgive us.

The congregation then says out loud, and the chazzan *repeats*

But You are the King, You are God Who lives forever!

וְאַתָּה הוּא מֶלֶךְ אֵל חַי וְקַיָּם.

Then the congregation continues here, and the chazzan *repeats after them*

There is no limit to Your years, there is no end to Your days. Who could possibly guess the number of Your heavenly chariots, who could possibly even understand Your Name? Your Name suits You, and You are worthy of Your Name. You have included Your Name within our own name (Yisrael).

Act for the sake of Your Name, make Your Name holy through the Jewish People who make Your name holy, because of the honor of Your great, holy Name — like the words of the holy angels who sanctify Your Name in Heaven. Together, the angels on high and people on earth announce three times the holiness of Your Name.

אֵין קִצְבָה לִשְׁנוֹתֶיךָ, וְאֵין קֵץ לְאֹרֶךְ יָמֶיךָ, וְאֵין לְשַׁעֵר מַרְכְּבוֹת כְּבוֹדֶךָ, וְאֵין לְפָרֵשׁ עֵלוּם שְׁמֶךָ. שִׁמְךָ נָאֶה לְךָ וְאַתָּה נָאֶה לִשְׁמֶךָ, וּשְׁמֵנוּ קָרָאתָ בִּשְׁמֶךָ.

עֲשֵׂה לְמַעַן שְׁמֶךָ, וְקַדֵּשׁ אֶת שִׁמְךָ עַל מַקְדִּישֵׁי שְׁמֶךָ, בַּעֲבוּר כְּבוֹד שִׁמְךָ הַנַּעֲרָץ וְהַנִּקְדָּשׁ, כְּסוֹד שִׂיחַ שַׂרְפֵי קֹדֶשׁ, הַמַּקְדִּישִׁים שִׁמְךָ בַּקֹּדֶשׁ, דָּרֵי מַעְלָה עִם דָּרֵי מַטָּה (קוֹרְאִים וּמְשַׁלְּשִׁים בְּשִׁלּוּשׁ קְדֻשָּׁה בַּקֹּדֶשׁ)

Did You Know??
Even if a person repents on the very last day of his life, he will be forgiven. Since we do not know when the last day of our life will be, we need to act properly and ask for forgiveness every single day.

Did You Know??
The purpose of this prayer is to show how our lives, at any given time, are held together by a tiny strand of thread, that can be ripped by Hashem at any time. We are in Hashem's hands completely, and we must learn to trust Him and do what He asks of us.

קְדוּשָׁה / Kedushah

The following *Kedushah* is recited at *Mussaf* of *Rosh Hashanah* and at all *Kedushos* of *Yom Kippur*.

As it is written by Your prophet: Each angel will call to another angel and say,

כַּכָּתוּב עַל יַד נְבִיאֶךָ, וְקָרָא זֶה אֶל זֶה וְאָמַר:

"Holy, holy, holy, Hashem, Master of the Heavenly bodies, the entire world is filled with His glory."

קָדוֹשׁ קָדוֹשׁ קָדוֹשׁ יהוה צְבָאוֹת, מְלֹא כָל הָאָרֶץ כְּבוֹדוֹ.

His glory fills the world. His angels ask each other, "Where is His place of glory?" The angels facing them answer, "Blessed …"

כְּבוֹדוֹ מָלֵא עוֹלָם, מְשָׁרְתָיו שׁוֹאֲלִים זֶה לָזֶה, אַיֵּה מְקוֹם כְּבוֹדוֹ, לְעֻמָּתָם בָּרוּךְ יֹאמֵרוּ:

"Blessed is the glory of Hashem from His Place."

בָּרוּךְ כְּבוֹד יהוה, מִמְּקוֹמוֹ.

From His place, may He turn with mercy and be compassionate to the people who declare that He is the One God. Every day, evening and morning, twice a day, with love, they say "Hear …"

מִמְּקוֹמוֹ הוּא יִפֶן בְּרַחֲמִים, וְיָחוֹן עַם הַמְיַחֲדִים שְׁמוֹ, עֶרֶב וָבֹקֶר בְּכָל יוֹם תָּמִיד, פַּעֲמַיִם בְּאַהֲבָה שְׁמַע אוֹמְרִים:

"Hear O Israel, Hashem is our God, Hashem is the only One."

שְׁמַע יִשְׂרָאֵל, יהוה אֱלֹהֵינוּ, יהוה אֶחָד.

He is our God. He is our Father. He is our King. He is our Savior. He will tell us with mercy for the second time in front of everything that is alive. "To be a God to you, I am Hashem, your God."

הוּא אֱלֹהֵינוּ, הוּא אָבִינוּ, הוּא מַלְכֵּנוּ, הוּא מוֹשִׁיעֵנוּ, וְהוּא יַשְׁמִיעֵנוּ בְּרַחֲמָיו שֵׁנִית, לְעֵינֵי כָּל חָי, לִהְיוֹת לָכֶם לֵאלֹהִים, אֲנִי יהוה אֱלֹהֵיכֶם.

Powerful is our mighty God. Hashem is our Master. Your Name is so powerful throughout the world. Hashem will be King over all the world. On that day (when *Mashiach* comes), He will be One and His Name will be One.

אַדִּיר אַדִּירֵנוּ, יהוה אֲדֹנֵנוּ, מָה אַדִּיר שִׁמְךָ בְּכָל הָאָרֶץ. וְהָיָה יהוה לְמֶלֶךְ עַל כָּל הָאָרֶץ, בַּיּוֹם הַהוּא יִהְיֶה יהוה אֶחָד וּשְׁמוֹ אֶחָד.

And in Your holy works it is written:

וּבְדִבְרֵי קָדְשְׁךָ כָּתוּב לֵאמֹר:

Hashem will be King forever. Your God, O Zion, from generation to generation. Halleluyah.

יִמְלֹךְ יהוה לְעוֹלָם, אֱלֹהַיִךְ צִיּוֹן לְדֹר וָדֹר, הַלְלוּיָהּ.

A Closer Look

The basic *Kedushah* prayer is said at least two times every day of the year. It is very holy and very ancient. It repeats the prayers that the angels in Heaven say in praise of Hashem every single day.

Did You Know??

We keep our feet together, just the way the angels stand — so it looks like they have one leg. When we say the words, "Holy, holy, holy," we lift ourselves up on our toes, trying to bring ourselves away from the earth and closer to Heaven.

Malchuyos   Zichronos   Shofaros

The next three sections of the davening are called *Malchuyos* (Kingship), 2. *Zichronos* (Remembrances) 3. *Shofaros* (Shofar Blasts).

מַלְכִיּוֹת / Malchuyos

We stand while reciting this prayer:

We should praise Hashem, the Master of everything, and speak of the greatness of He Who created everything. For He did not make us like the other nations and He did not make us like the families of the world. He did not make our share like theirs. They bow down and pray to a god that cannot help them.

עָלֵינוּ לְשַׁבֵּחַ לַאֲדוֹן הַכֹּל, לָתֵת גְּדֻלָּה לְיוֹצֵר בְּרֵאשִׁית, שֶׁלֹּא עָשָׂנוּ כְּגוֹיֵי הָאֲרָצוֹת, וְלֹא שָׂמָנוּ כְּמִשְׁפְּחוֹת הָאֲדָמָה. שֶׁלֹּא שָׂם חֶלְקֵנוּ כָּהֶם, וְגוֹרָלֵנוּ כְּכָל הֲמוֹנָם. שֶׁהֵם מִשְׁתַּחֲוִים לְהֶבֶל וָרִיק, וּמִתְפַּלְּלִים אֶל אֵל לֹא יוֹשִׁיעַ.

We bow with our knees and hands on the floor while reciting וַאֲנַחְנוּ כּוֹרְעִים וּמִשְׁתַּחֲוִים.

But we bow and give thanks to the King of all kings, the Holy One, blessed is He. Hashem spreads out the heavens and establishes the earth. Hashem is in Heaven. He is our God, there is no other. Our King is true, there is no other besides Him. As it is written in His Torah: "You will know this day, and realize it in your heart, that Hashem is the only God in the Heavens above and on the earth below. There is no other."

וַאֲנַחְנוּ כּוֹרְעִים וּמִשְׁתַּחֲוִים וּמוֹדִים, לִפְנֵי מֶלֶךְ מַלְכֵי הַמְּלָכִים, הַקָּדוֹשׁ בָּרוּךְ הוּא. שֶׁהוּא נוֹטֶה שָׁמַיִם וְיוֹסֵד אָרֶץ, וּמוֹשַׁב יְקָרוֹ בַּשָּׁמַיִם מִמַּעַל, וּשְׁכִינַת עֻזּוֹ בְּגָבְהֵי מְרוֹמִים, הוּא אֱלֹהֵינוּ, אֵין עוֹד. אֱמֶת מַלְכֵּנוּ, אֶפֶס זוּלָתוֹ, כַּכָּתוּב בְּתוֹרָתוֹ: וְיָדַעְתָּ הַיּוֹם וַהֲשֵׁבֹתָ אֶל לְבָבֶךָ, כִּי יהוה הוּא הָאֱלֹהִים בַּשָּׁמַיִם מִמַּעַל וְעַל הָאָרֶץ מִתָּחַת, אֵין עוֹד.

A Closer Look

Aleinu begins the section of the davening called מַלְכִיּוֹת, Kingship. מַלְכִיּוֹת is a section which contains Torah verses describing that Hashem is King. After the *chazzan* finishes the section, we blow the shofar.

Did You Know??

Jews do not usually bow down on their knees. An exception to this is on Rosh Hashanah and Yom Kippur. This is because of the special holiness of the day.

Did You Know??

The Midrash tells us that *Aleinu* was composed by Yehoshua after he led the Jews across the Jordan River into Eretz Yisrael.

Did You Know??

We are not allowed to bow down on our knees on a floor outside the *Beis HaMikdash*. Therefore, when we bow on our knees during *Aleinu*, we make sure to put something (a towel or paper) under our knees so that we do not directly touch the floor.

פְּסוּקֵי מַלְכִיּוֹת / The Verses of Malchuyos

Each of the following sections (*Malchuyos, Zichronos, Shofaros*) is divided into ten verses —
three from the Torah, three from *Nevi'im* (Prophets), three from *Kesuvim* (Writings), and the tenth from the Torah.

As it is written in Your Torah:

1. "Hashem will rule forever"

2. And it is said: "He sees no sin in Yaakov (the Jewish people) and sees no evil plans in Israel. Hashem, his God, is with Israel, and the affection of the King (Hashem) is with it."

3. And it is said: "And He became King in Israel, when all the people assembled and joined together."

And in Your Holy Writings (*Kesuvim*) it is written:

4. "For the Kingship is His, and He rules all the nations."

5. And it says: "Hashem has ruled, He put on grandeur, He will wear His Power, and has made the world strong so it will not fall."

6. And it says: "Open up, gates, be uplifted, so that the King of Glory may enter. Who is the King of Glory? Hashem, Who is strong and mighty, Hashem Who is powerful in war. Open up, gates, so that the King of Glory may enter. Who is the King of Glory? Hashem, the Master of Armies, the King of Honor, *Selah*."

And by Your servants, the Prophets, it is written:

7. "Hashem, the King and Redeemer of Israel said, 'I am the first, and I am the last. There is no other God.'"

8. And it says: "The saviors will go up to Har Tziyon, and they will judge the descendants of Eisav, and Hashem will rule."

9. And it says: "Then Hashem will be King over all the world; on that day (the Day of Judgment) Hashem will be One, and His Name will be One."

10. And in Your Torah it is written: "Hear, O Israel, Hashem is our God, Hashem is the only One."

כַּכָּתוּב בְּתוֹרָתֶךָ: יהוה יִמְלֹךְ לְעֹלָם וָעֶד. וְנֶאֱמַר: לֹא הִבִּיט אָוֶן בְּיַעֲקֹב, וְלֹא רָאָה עָמָל בְּיִשְׂרָאֵל; יהוה אֱלֹהָיו עִמּוֹ, וּתְרוּעַת מֶלֶךְ בּוֹ. וְנֶאֱמַר: וַיְהִי בִישֻׁרוּן מֶלֶךְ, בְּהִתְאַסֵּף רָאשֵׁי עָם, יַחַד שִׁבְטֵי יִשְׂרָאֵל.

וּבְדִבְרֵי קָדְשְׁךָ כָּתוּב לֵאמֹר: כִּי לַיהוה הַמְּלוּכָה וּמֹשֵׁל בַּגּוֹיִם. וְנֶאֱמַר: יהוה מָלָךְ גֵּאוּת לָבֵשׁ, לָבֵשׁ יהוה, עֹז הִתְאַזָּר, אַף תִּכּוֹן תֵּבֵל בַּל תִּמּוֹט. וְנֶאֱמַר: שְׂאוּ שְׁעָרִים רָאשֵׁיכֶם, וְהִנָּשְׂאוּ פִּתְחֵי עוֹלָם, וְיָבוֹא מֶלֶךְ הַכָּבוֹד. מִי זֶה מֶלֶךְ הַכָּבוֹד, יהוה עִזּוּז וְגִבּוֹר, יהוה גִּבּוֹר מִלְחָמָה. שְׂאוּ שְׁעָרִים רָאשֵׁיכֶם, וּשְׂאוּ פִּתְחֵי עוֹלָם, וְיָבֹא מֶלֶךְ הַכָּבוֹד. מִי הוּא זֶה מֶלֶךְ הַכָּבוֹד, יהוה צְבָאוֹת, הוּא מֶלֶךְ הַכָּבוֹד סֶלָה.

וְעַל יְדֵי עֲבָדֶיךָ הַנְּבִיאִים כָּתוּב לֵאמֹר: כֹּה אָמַר יהוה, מֶלֶךְ יִשְׂרָאֵל וְגֹאֲלוֹ, יהוה צְבָאוֹת, אֲנִי רִאשׁוֹן וַאֲנִי אַחֲרוֹן, וּמִבַּלְעָדַי אֵין אֱלֹהִים. וְנֶאֱמַר: וְעָלוּ מוֹשִׁיעִים בְּהַר צִיּוֹן לִשְׁפֹּט אֶת הַר עֵשָׂו, וְהָיְתָה לַיהוה הַמְּלוּכָה. וְנֶאֱמַר: וְהָיָה יהוה לְמֶלֶךְ עַל כָּל הָאָרֶץ, בַּיּוֹם הַהוּא יִהְיֶה יהוה אֶחָד וּשְׁמוֹ אֶחָד. וּבְתוֹרָתְךָ כָּתוּב לֵאמֹר: שְׁמַע יִשְׂרָאֵל, יהוה אֱלֹהֵינוּ, יהוה אֶחָד.

A Closer Look
We mention "On that day." This refers to the Final Day of Judgment when the entire world will be judged by Hashem.

Everyone now stands and the shofar is blown:

Tekiah, Shevarim-Teruah, Tekiah,

Tekiah, Shevarim, Tekiah,

Tekiah, Teruah, Tekiah.

תְּקִיעָה. שְׁבָרִים-תְּרוּעָה. תְּקִיעָה.

תְּקִיעָה. שְׁבָרִים. תְּקִיעָה.

תְּקִיעָה. תְּרוּעָה. תְּקִיעָה.

Everyone now says הַיּוֹם הֲרַת עוֹלָם found on page 50.

A Closer Look

This section talks about how Hashem rules the entire world. This means that nothing in the world happens without Hashem decreeing that it should happen.

פְּסוּקֵי זִכְרוֹנוֹת / The Verses of Zichronos

As it is written in Your Torah:

1. "Hashem remembered Noach and all the animals and living things that were with him in the Ark. Hashem sent a spirit to pass over the world and all the waters went down."

2. And it is said: "And Hashem heard their groans (in the land of Egypt). And He heard that, he remembered His agreement with Avraham, with Yitzchak, and with Yaakov."

3. And it is said: "I will remember my agreement with Yaakov, and my agreement with Yitzchak, and my agreement with Avraham — and I will remember the Land (Eretz Yisrael)."

And in Your Holy Writings (*Kesuvim*) it is written:

4. "He made a memorial of His wonders (reminders of what He did for us), for Hashem is compassionate."

5. And it is said: "He gave food for those who fear Him. He remembers his agreement forever."

6. And it is said: "He remembered his agreement for them, and saved them, because He is so kind."

By Your servants, the Prophets, it is written:

7. "Go and call out, 'Hashem said, "I remember how you (the Nation of Israel) were kind when you were young, the love you had, how you followed Me in the desert, a land that was not yet planted."'"

8. And it is said: "I will remember My agreement with you, from when you were young, and I will make this an agreement forever."

9. And it is said: "'The Jewish People are my most loved child. Whenever I speak of them, don't I remember them more and more? Therefore, I will take pity on them.' These are the words of Hashem."

כַּכָּתוּב בְּתוֹרָתֶךָ: וַיִּזְכֹּר אֱלֹהִים אֶת נֹחַ, וְאֵת כָּל הַחַיָּה וְאֶת כָּל הַבְּהֵמָה אֲשֶׁר אִתּוֹ בַּתֵּבָה, וַיַּעֲבֵר אֱלֹהִים רוּחַ עַל הָאָרֶץ, וַיָּשֹׁכּוּ הַמָּיִם. וְנֶאֱמַר: וַיִּשְׁמַע אֱלֹהִים אֶת נַאֲקָתָם, וַיִּזְכֹּר אֱלֹהִים אֶת בְּרִיתוֹ אֶת אַבְרָהָם, אֶת יִצְחָק וְאֶת יַעֲקֹב. וְנֶאֱמַר: וְזָכַרְתִּי אֶת בְּרִיתִי יַעֲקוֹב, וְאַף אֶת בְּרִיתִי יִצְחָק, וְאַף אֶת בְּרִיתִי אַבְרָהָם אֶזְכֹּר, וְהָאָרֶץ אֶזְכֹּר.

וּבְדִבְרֵי קָדְשְׁךָ כָּתוּב לֵאמֹר: זֵכֶר עָשָׂה לְנִפְלְאֹתָיו, חַנּוּן וְרַחוּם יהוה. וְנֶאֱמַר: טֶרֶף נָתַן לִירֵאָיו, יִזְכֹּר לְעוֹלָם בְּרִיתוֹ. וְנֶאֱמַר: וַיִּזְכֹּר לָהֶם בְּרִיתוֹ, וַיִּנָּחֵם כְּרֹב חֲסָדָיו.

וְעַל יְדֵי עֲבָדֶיךָ הַנְּבִיאִים כָּתוּב לֵאמֹר: הָלֹךְ וְקָרָאתָ בְאָזְנֵי יְרוּשָׁלַיִם לֵאמֹר, כֹּה אָמַר יהוה, זָכַרְתִּי לָךְ חֶסֶד נְעוּרַיִךְ, אַהֲבַת כְּלוּלֹתָיִךְ, לֶכְתֵּךְ אַחֲרַי בַּמִּדְבָּר, בְּאֶרֶץ לֹא זְרוּעָה. וְנֶאֱמַר: וְזָכַרְתִּי אֲנִי אֶת בְּרִיתִי אוֹתָךְ בִּימֵי נְעוּרָיִךְ, וַהֲקִימוֹתִי לָךְ בְּרִית עוֹלָם. וְנֶאֱמַר: הֲבֵן יַקִּיר לִי אֶפְרַיִם, אִם יֶלֶד שַׁעֲשֻׁעִים, כִּי מִדֵּי דַבְּרִי בּוֹ זָכֹר אֶזְכְּרֶנּוּ עוֹד, עַל כֵּן הָמוּ מֵעַי לוֹ, רַחֵם אֲרַחֲמֶנּוּ, נְאֻם יהוה.

A Closer Look

We hope that in the same way Hashem remembered all these things that He has already done for us, He will also remember to be merciful to us on this Day of Judgment.

46

10. As it is said: "And I shall remember for their sake the agreement I made with their forefathers, whom I took out of Egypt in front of the entire world, to be their God. I am Hashem."

כָּאֲמוּר: וְזָכַרְתִּי לָהֶם בְּרִית רִאשׁוֹנִים, אֲשֶׁר הוֹצֵאתִי אֹתָם מֵאֶרֶץ מִצְרַיִם לְעֵינֵי הַגּוֹיִם לִהְיוֹת לָהֶם לֵאלֹהִים, אֲנִי יהוה.

Everyone now stands and the shofar is blown:

Tekiah, Shevarim-Teruah, Tekiah,

Tekiah, Shevarim, Tekiah,

Tekiah, Teruah, Tekiah.

תקיעה. שברים־תרועה. תקיעה.

תקיעה. שברים. תקיעה.

תקיעה. תרועה. תקיעה.

Everyone now says הַיּוֹם הֲרַת עוֹלָם found on page 50.

A Closer Look

This section talks about many different things that Hashem remembered: 1. Noach. 2. Bringing the Jewish People out of Egypt. 3. Bringing the Jews back to Eretz Yisrael. 4. He gave us reminders of His Kindness to remind us of Him. 5. He gave us food in the desert, 6. He remembered all He promised to us and saved us from many persecutions. 7-9. How the Jewish People loved Hashem and followed Him through the desert into Eretz Yisrael. 10. He remembers the agreement He made with our forefathers.

47

פְּסוּקֵי שׁוֹפְרוֹת / The Verses of Shofaros

As it is written in Your Torah:

1. "And it was on the third day, when it was morning, there was thunder and lightning, a heavy cloud was on the mountain, and the sound of the shofar was very loud and strong, and all the people in the camp trembled."

2. And it is said: "And the sound of the shofar became stronger and stronger. Moshe would speak and Hashem would answer with a voice."

3. And it is said: "All the people saw the sounds and the flames and the sound of the shofar, and the smoking mountain. And all the people saw this and trembled and stood far away."

And in Your Holy Writings (*Kesuvim*) it is written:

4. "Hashem went up with the blast of the shofar."

5. And it is said: "With trumpets and the blast from the shofar, you should call out before Hashem, the King."

6. And it is said: "Blow the shofar at the beginning of this new month, at the time of our holiday, because it is a law for Jewish People to do so, a Judgment Day for Hashem."

By Your servants, the Prophets, it is written:

7. "All the people of the earth will see that the Jewish People have been gathered together, as if a flag were raised high on the mountains. And you will hear it as if a shofar has been blown."

8. And it is said: "And it will be on that day, a great shofar will be blown and all the Jewish people who have been lost throughout the world will come back, and will bow down to Hashem on the holy mountain in Yerushalayim."

כַּכָּתוּב בְּתוֹרָתֶךָ: וַיְהִי בַיּוֹם הַשְּׁלִישִׁי בִּהְיֹת הַבֹּקֶר, וַיְהִי קֹלֹת וּבְרָקִים, וְעָנָן כָּבֵד עַל הָהָר, וְקֹל שֹׁפָר חָזָק מְאֹד, וַיֶּחֱרַד כָּל הָעָם אֲשֶׁר בַּמַּחֲנֶה. וְנֶאֱמַר: וַיְהִי קוֹל הַשֹּׁפָר הוֹלֵךְ וְחָזֵק מְאֹד, מֹשֶׁה יְדַבֵּר וְהָאֱלֹהִים יַעֲנֶנּוּ בְקוֹל. וְנֶאֱמַר: וְכָל הָעָם רֹאִים אֶת הַקּוֹלֹת, וְאֶת הַלַּפִּידִם, וְאֵת קוֹל הַשֹּׁפָר, וְאֶת הָהָר עָשֵׁן; וַיַּרְא הָעָם וַיָּנֻעוּ, וַיַּעַמְדוּ מֵרָחֹק.

וּבְדִבְרֵי קָדְשְׁךָ כָּתוּב לֵאמֹר: עָלָה אֱלֹהִים בִּתְרוּעָה, יהוה בְּקוֹל שׁוֹפָר. וְנֶאֱמַר: בַּחֲצֹצְרוֹת וְקוֹל שׁוֹפָר הָרִיעוּ לִפְנֵי הַמֶּלֶךְ יהוה. וְנֶאֱמַר: תִּקְעוּ בַחֹדֶשׁ שׁוֹפָר, בַּכֶּסֶה לְיוֹם חַגֵּנוּ. כִּי חֹק לְיִשְׂרָאֵל הוּא, מִשְׁפָּט לֵאלֹהֵי יַעֲקֹב.

וְעַל יְדֵי עֲבָדֶיךָ הַנְּבִיאִים כָּתוּב לֵאמֹר: כָּל יֹשְׁבֵי תֵבֵל וְשֹׁכְנֵי אָרֶץ, כִּנְשֹׂא נֵס הָרִים תִּרְאוּ, וְכִתְקֹעַ שׁוֹפָר תִּשְׁמָעוּ. וְנֶאֱמַר: וְהָיָה בַּיּוֹם הַהוּא יִתָּקַע בְּשׁוֹפָר גָּדוֹל, וּבָאוּ הָאֹבְדִים בְּאֶרֶץ אַשּׁוּר, וְהַנִּדָּחִים בְּאֶרֶץ מִצְרָיִם, וְהִשְׁתַּחֲווּ לַיהוה בְּהַר הַקֹּדֶשׁ בִּירוּשָׁלָיִם.

Did You Know??
Many miracles were brought about by the blowing of the shofar. For example, the walls of the city of Yericho fell after Yehoshua had shofars blown.

Did You Know??
On that great Judgment Day in the future, the shofar will be blown, *Mashiach* will arrive, and all the Jews will be brought back to Eretz Yisrael to worship Hashem there, in the *Beis HaMikdash*.

9. And it is said: "And Hashem will appear to them, and His arrow will fly like a streak of lightning, and Hashem will sound the shofar, and He will fight the armies in the south, and He will protect them." Protect us, too, with your peace.

וְנֶאֱמַר: וַיהוה עֲלֵיהֶם יֵרָאֶה, וְיָצָא כַבָּרָק חִצּוֹ, וַאדֹנָי יֱהוִה בַּשּׁוֹפָר יִתְקָע, וְהָלַךְ בְּסַעֲרוֹת תֵּימָן. יהוה צְבָאוֹת יָגֵן עֲלֵיהֶם. כֵּן תָּגֵן עַל עַמְּךָ יִשְׂרָאֵל בִּשְׁלוֹמֶךָ.

10. As it is said: "On the day of your joy, on your festivals, and on the new moons, you are to blow the trumpets, when you bring sacrfices. These shall be a remembrance before Hashem. I am Hashem, your God."

כָּאמוּר: וּבְיוֹם שִׂמְחַתְכֶם וּבְמוֹעֲדֵיכֶם וּבְרָאשֵׁי חָדְשֵׁיכֶם, וּתְקַעְתֶּם בַּחֲצֹצְרֹת עַל עֹלֹתֵיכֶם וְעַל זִבְחֵי שַׁלְמֵיכֶם; וְהָיוּ לָכֶם לְזִכָּרוֹן לִפְנֵי אֱלֹהֵיכֶם, אֲנִי יהוה אֱלֹהֵיכֶם.

Everyone now stands and the shofar is blown:

Tekiah, Shevarim-Teruah, Tekiah,

Tekiah, Shevarim, Tekiah,

Tekiah, Teruah, Tekiah.

תְּקִיעָה. שְׁבָרִים־תְּרוּעָה. תְּקִיעָה.

תְּקִיעָה. שְׁבָרִים. תְּקִיעָה.

תְּקִיעָה. תְּרוּעָה. תְּקִיעָה.

Everyone now says הַיּוֹם הֲרַת עוֹלָם found on page 50.

A Closer Look
This part of the davening, *Shofaros*, begins with the story of how the shofar was blown when the Jewish People received the Torah at Har Sinai.

Did You Know??
The last verse does not mention a shofar — but it is included in our group of ten verses because it does mention blowing an instrument before Hashem.

הַיוֹם הֲרַת עוֹלָם / Hayom Haras Olam

Today is the birthday of the world. Today, all people that Hashem created stand in judgment — both as His children and as His servants. If we are as children, please have mercy like a father on his children. And if we are as servants, we long for You to be gracious to us, and give us a good verdict, O awesome Holy God.

הַיוֹם הֲרַת עוֹלָם, הַיוֹם יַעֲמִיד בַּמִּשְׁפָּט כָּל יְצוּרֵי עוֹלָמִים, אִם כְּבָנִים, אִם כַּעֲבָדִים. אִם כְּבָנִים, רַחֲמֵנוּ כְּרַחֵם אָב עַל בָּנִים. וְאִם כַּעֲבָדִים, עֵינֵינוּ לְךָ תְלוּיוֹת, עַד שֶׁתְּחָנֵּנוּ וְתוֹצִיא כָאוֹר מִשְׁפָּטֵנוּ, אָיוֹם קָדוֹשׁ.

אֲרֶשֶׁת שְׂפָתֵינוּ / Areshes Sefaseinu

May our words be pleasant to You, O God in Heaven. You are the One Who understands and listens, Who looks closely and hears the sounds of the shofar. May You accept our prayers with mercy.

אֲרֶשֶׁת שְׂפָתֵינוּ יֶעֱרַב לְפָנֶיךָ, אֵל רָם וְנִשָּׂא, מֵבִין וּמַאֲזִין, מַבִּיט וּמַקְשִׁיב לְקוֹל תְּקִיעָתֵנוּ. וּתְקַבֵּל בְּרַחֲמִים וּבְרָצוֹן סֵדֶר שׁוֹפְרוֹתֵינוּ.

Did You Know??
Rosh Hashanah traditionally celebrates the creation of the world. The Torah refers to the month of Nissan as the first month of the year because that is when the Jewish people left Egypt, and became the Jewish nation.

According to some Sages, the world was actually created in Nissan. Some explain that Hashem decided to create the world on Rosh Hashanah, but He actually created it later, in Nissan.

Did You Know??
Rosh Hashanah does not commemorate the first day of the creation of the world. Rosh Hashanah commemorates the sixth day of creation, the day that Hashem created Man. The sixth day of creation is referred to as the beginning of creation because Man is the reason everything else was created. The world was created so Man would carry out the will of Hashem.

בִּרְכַּת כֹּהֲנִים / The Kohanim's Blessing

The *chazzan* or *gabbai* calls out aloud:

Kohanim!!!

The Kohanim say:

Blessed are You, Hashem, our God, King of the universe, Who makes us holy with the holiness of Aharon, and has commanded us to bless His people with love.

בָּרוּךְ אַתָּה יהוה אֱלֹהֵינוּ מֶלֶךְ הָעוֹלָם, אֲשֶׁר קִדְּשָׁנוּ בִּקְדֻשָּׁתוֹ שֶׁל אַהֲרֹן, וְצִוָּנוּ לְבָרֵךְ אֶת עַמּוֹ יִשְׂרָאֵל בְּאַהֲבָה.

The *chazzan* calls out each of the following words, and they are then repeated by the Kohanim:

May He bless you —	יְבָרֶכְךָ	May He turn —	יִשָּׂא
Hashem —	יהוה	Hashem —	יהוה
And watch over you.	וְיִשְׁמְרֶךָ.	His Face	פָּנָיו

Everyone answers:
Amen. אָמֵן.

May He shine —	יָאֵר	Toward you	אֵלֶיךָ
Hashem —	יהוה	And establish	וְיָשֵׂם
His Face	פָּנָיו	For you	לְךָ
Toward you	אֵלֶיךָ	Peace	שָׁלוֹם.
And grant you grace.	וִיחֻנֶּךָ.		

Everyone answers:
Amen. אָמֵן.

Everyone answers:
Amen. אָמֵן.

Did You Know??
Until the time of the *Avos* (Avraham, Yitzchak and Yaakov), Hashem, Himself, directly blessed the people. Then Hashem gave this power to bless the people to Avraham, Yitzchak, and Yaakov. After they died, Hashem blesses the Jewish people through the Kohanim.

A Closer Look
When the Kohanim raise their arms under the tallis to bless the people, it is as if the blessing of Hashem goes from Him, through the hands of the Kohanim, directly to the Jewish people. This means that the blessing is not from the Kohanim, but it is Hashem using the Kohanim as His instrument to send His blessing *through* them, to the people.

הַיּוֹם / *Hayom*

The congregation and then the *chazzan* say the first phrase.
Everyone responds *Amen* after the *chazzan*, and then says the next phrase.

Today, please strengthen us.	Amen	אָמֵן. הַיּוֹם תְּאַמְּצֵנוּ.
Today, please bless us.	Amen	אָמֵן. הַיּוֹם תְּבָרְכֵנוּ.
Today, please make us great.	Amen	אָמֵן. הַיּוֹם תְּגַדְּלֵנוּ.
Today, please see only good in us.	Amen	אָמֵן. הַיּוֹם תִּדְרְשֵׁנוּ לְטוֹבָה.
Today, please hear our cry to You.	Amen	אָמֵן. הַיּוֹם תִּשְׁמַע שַׁוְעָתֵנוּ.
Today, please accept our prayers with kindness. Amen		הַיּוֹם תְּקַבֵּל בְּרַחֲמִים וּבְרָצוֹן אֶת תְּפִלָּתֵנוּ. אָמֵן.
Today, support us with Your strength and righteousness. Amen		אָמֵן. הַיּוֹם תִּתְמְכֵנוּ בִּימִין צִדְקֶךָ.

A Closer Look
We can really pray even using our own words, but the Sages who wrote the *Machzor* knew what is the best way for our words to reach Hashem.

A Closer Look
On Rosh Hashanah, when Hashem is sitting in judgment of us, we beg Him directly with these prayers to judge us favorably.

Did You Know??
The first four sentences are in alphabetical order. Some *Machzorim* go through the entire alphabet with similar prayers.

לְדָוִד / L'David

We have been reciting this psalm at the end of davening during the entire month of Elul and will do so during Tishrei until Shemini Atzeres. This psalm helps us prepare for Rosh Hashanah and Yom Kippur. David is sad about things he has done wrong. He repents and begs Hashem for forgiveness.

For David: Hashem is my Light and my Salvation. (And so,) of whom should I be afraid? He is the strength of my life, and so, whom (besides Him) should I fear? When evil people come close to me to destroy me — those people who are my enemies — they shall fall and be defeated. Even if an army were standing against me, I would not be afraid. Even if a war were started against me, I would trust in Hashem. I have asked only one thing from Hashem, this is what I seek: To live in the House of Hashem, all the days of my life. I wish that I could see the sweetness of Hashem, and to go to His Temple each morning. He will hide me in His Shelter, on a very bad day. He will hide me in His safe place, He will lift me up on a rock (to safety). Now, I am lifted up higher than all my enemies who are around me. I will bring offerings to Him in His Temple with joyous song. I will sing praises to Hashem. Hear my voice when I call to You, Hashem. Be very kind to me, answer me. Deep in my heart I am told by You, "Look for Me, seek Me out." Hashem, I will look for You. Do not hide Yourself from me. Do not send me away in anger. You have always been the One Who helped me. Do not forget me. Do not abandon me. You are the One Who saves me. Even if my father and my mother have forgotten about me, You, Hashem, will bring me close to You. Hashem, teach me Your Ways. Lead me on the path of righteousness, because of my enemies who always watch me. Do not do to me what my enemies wish. Liars speak against me, saying things about me that cause me trouble. But I believed I would see the goodness of Hashem in this world. Hope to Hashem. Be strong, He will give you courage. Always hope to Hashem.

לְדָוִד, יהוה אוֹרִי וְיִשְׁעִי, מִמִּי אִירָא, יהוה מָעוֹז חַיַּי, מִמִּי אֶפְחָד. בִּקְרֹב עָלַי מְרֵעִים לֶאֱכֹל אֶת בְּשָׂרִי, צָרַי וְאֹיְבַי לִי, הֵמָּה כָשְׁלוּ וְנָפָלוּ. אִם תַּחֲנֶה עָלַי מַחֲנֶה, לֹא יִירָא לִבִּי, אִם תָּקוּם עָלַי מִלְחָמָה, בְּזֹאת אֲנִי בוֹטֵחַ. אַחַת שָׁאַלְתִּי מֵאֵת יהוה, אוֹתָהּ אֲבַקֵּשׁ, שִׁבְתִּי בְּבֵית יהוה כָּל יְמֵי חַיַּי, לַחֲזוֹת בְּנֹעַם יהוה, וּלְבַקֵּר בְּהֵיכָלוֹ. כִּי יִצְפְּנֵנִי בְּסֻכֹּה בְּיוֹם רָעָה, יַסְתִּרֵנִי בְּסֵתֶר אָהֳלוֹ, בְּצוּר יְרוֹמְמֵנִי. וְעַתָּה יָרוּם רֹאשִׁי עַל אֹיְבַי סְבִיבוֹתַי, וְאֶזְבְּחָה בְאָהֳלוֹ זִבְחֵי תְרוּעָה, אָשִׁירָה וַאֲזַמְּרָה לַיהוה. שְׁמַע יהוה קוֹלִי אֶקְרָא, וְחָנֵּנִי וַעֲנֵנִי. לְךָ אָמַר לִבִּי בַּקְּשׁוּ פָנָי, אֶת פָּנֶיךָ יהוה אֲבַקֵּשׁ. אַל תַּסְתֵּר פָּנֶיךָ מִמֶּנִּי, אַל תַּט בְּאַף עַבְדֶּךָ, עֶזְרָתִי הָיִיתָ, אַל תִּטְּשֵׁנִי וְאַל תַּעַזְבֵנִי, אֱלֹהֵי יִשְׁעִי. כִּי אָבִי וְאִמִּי עֲזָבוּנִי, וַיהוה יַאַסְפֵנִי. הוֹרֵנִי יהוה דַּרְכֶּךָ, וּנְחֵנִי בְּאֹרַח מִישׁוֹר, לְמַעַן שׁוֹרְרָי. אַל תִּתְּנֵנִי בְּנֶפֶשׁ צָרָי, כִּי קָמוּ בִי עֵדֵי שֶׁקֶר, וִיפֵחַ חָמָס. לוּלֵא הֶאֱמַנְתִּי לִרְאוֹת בְּטוּב יהוה בְּאֶרֶץ חַיִּים. קַוֵּה אֶל יהוה, חֲזַק וְיַאֲמֵץ לִבֶּךָ, וְקַוֵּה אֶל יהוה.

A Closer Look

David has placed his total trust in Hashem. He places his life in Hashem's Hands. He trusts Hashem, and therefore fears no man. He fully trusts that Hashem will keep him safe. He says that his only true desire is to be close to Hashem, to understand Hashem's Laws, and to pray in Hashem's Temple. He knows that as long as he is in Hashem's Temple he is truly safe.

At the end, he explains to everyone that they, also, need to have full faith in Hashem.

Did You Know??

"On a very bad day" (verse 5) refers to the day the wicked Queen Ataliah murdered and wiped out almost all of King David's descendants. But she did not know about one infant child, Yoash. Yoash's aunt hid him in an attic above the Holy of Holies for six years, and saved him from the murderous Ataliah. Yoash grew up to become the king.

David is praying here that Hashem will save Yoash and all his descendants.

תַּשְׁלִיךְ / *Tashlich*

On the first afternoon of Rosh Hashanah, after Minchah, we go to a body of water and recite *Tashlich*.
If the first day of Rosh Hashanah comes out on Shabbos, we say *Tashlich* on the second day of Rosh Hashanah.
If there is no place within walking distance, *Tashlich* can be said during the *Aseres Yemei Teshuvah*, or even until Hoshanah Rabbah.

מִי אֵל כָּמֽוֹךָ נֹשֵׂא עָוֹן וְעֹבֵר עַל פֶּשַׁע לִשְׁאֵרִית נַחֲלָתוֹ לֹא הֶחֱזִיק לָעַד אַפּוֹ כִּי חָפֵץ חֶסֶד הוּא. יָשׁוּב יְרַחֲמֵנוּ יִכְבֹּשׁ עֲוֹנֹתֵֽינוּ וְתַשְׁלִיךְ בִּמְצֻלוֹת יָם כָּל חַטֹּאתָם.

(וְכָל חַטֹּאת עַמְּךָ בֵּית יִשְׂרָאֵל, תַּשְׁלִיךְ בִּמְקוֹם אֲשֶׁר לֹא יִזָּכְרוּ, וְלֹא יִפָּקְדוּ, וְלֹא יַעֲלוּ עַל לֵב לְעוֹלָם.)

תִּתֵּן אֱמֶת לְיַעֲקֹב חֶסֶד לְאַבְרָהָם אֲשֶׁר נִשְׁבַּֽעְתָּ לַאֲבֹתֵֽינוּ מִֽימֵי קֶֽדֶם.

God, Who is like You, Who forgives the sins of the Jewish people. He doesn't hold on to His anger for a long time, because He desires to do kindness. He will always show mercy to us; He will hide our sins. And throw all the sins of the Jewish nation into the deepest ocean.
(All the sins of Your Jewish people You will throw into a place where they will not be remembered, and never come to mind again.)

You will keep Your promise to Yaakov, be kind to Avraham, just as You promised our ancestors long ago.

We now say the following verses from *Tehillim*:

מִן הַמֵּצַר קָרָֽאתִי יָּהּ עָנָֽנִי בַמֶּרְחָב יָהּ. יהוה לִי לֹא אִירָא מַה יַּעֲשֶׂה לִי אָדָם. יהוה לִי בְּעֹזְרָי וַאֲנִי אֶרְאֶה בְשֹׂנְאָי. טוֹב לַחֲסוֹת בַּיהוה, מִבְּטֹחַ בָּאָדָם. טוֹב לַחֲסוֹת בַּיהוה, מִבְּטֹחַ בִּנְדִיבִים.

From my troubles I called to Hashem and He answered me generously. Hashem is with me, I have no fear — what can man do to me? Hashem is with me, through my helpers, and therefore I can face my enemies. It is better to take protection from Hashem, than to count on man. It is better to take protection from Hashem than to rely on rulers.

Did You Know??

In ancient times, when a man was declared a king, it was usually done at a riverbank. On Rosh Hashanah, we declare that Hashem is our King, and we do this near a body of water.

Also, when Avraham was bringing Yitzchak to be sacrificed on Har Moriah, the evil Satan tried to stop him. He went in front of Avraham, turning himself into a giant river to drown Avraham and Yitzchak, but they had faith in Hashem and kept going. Hashem stopped the Satan and saved Avraham and Yitzchak. Since the *Akeidah* happened on Rosh Hashanah (see pages 30-32), we say the *Tashlich* prayers by a body of water.

A Closer Look

It would be silly to think that we could take our sins and just throw them away into water. There is only one way we can get rid of our sins, and that is to do *teshuvah*. Hope is that by the time we say *Tashlich*, we have already done *teshuvah*. We are taking those sins that have already been forgiven and "throwing them away." We are saying that we will try never to do these sins again and we are asking Hashem to forgive us.

Did You Know??

When *Tashlich* is said on a weekday, some have the custom to take crumbs of bread and throw them into the water. We are symbolically throwing our sins away, to a place they will never again be found.

כַּפָּרוֹת / *Kaparos*

We may perform *Kaparos* anytime between Rosh Hashanah and Yom Kippur. But the preferred time to perform it is at dawn on Erev Yom Kippur. We perform *Kaparos* with either a chicken that will be given to charity (as food for the poor) or with money that is given to charity. When using a chicken, men and boys use a rooster and women and girls use a hen.

The following is said three times:

People sit in darkness, in the shadow of death, chained up in terror. Hashem will remove them from darkness and the shadow of death, and will break open their chains.

בְּנֵי אָדָם יֹשְׁבֵי חֹשֶׁךְ וְצַלְמָוֶת, אֲסִירֵי עֳנִי וּבַרְזֶל. יוֹצִיאֵם מֵחֹשֶׁךְ וְצַלְמָוֶת, וּמוֹסְרוֹתֵיהֶם יְנַתֵּק.

The chicken or the money is held and waved in a circular motion over one's head as the following prayer is said:

This is a substitute for me, this is an atonement for me. This chicken will go to its death (if using money: this money will go to charity) while I will have a good, long, and peaceful life.

זֶה חֲלִיפָתִי, זֶה תְּמוּרָתִי, זֶה כַּפָּרָתִי. זֶה הַתַּרְנְגוֹל יֵלֵךְ לְמִיתָה [זֶה הַכֶּסֶף יֵלֵךְ לִצְדָקָה], וַאֲנִי אֶכָּנֵס וְאֵלֵךְ לְחַיִּים טוֹבִים אֲרֻכִים וּלְשָׁלוֹם.

A Closer Look

We say *Kaparos* to make us realize that we are being judged by Hashem and our very life is in danger. Just as the chicken's life will be taken away, so too, our life can also be taken away. After the chicken is killed, it is given to a poor family, or the money is given to the poor, because charity is an important part of *teshuvah* (repentance).

Did You Know??

We use a chicken for *Kaparos* instead of a different animal so that no one will think that we are sacrificing an animal, since a sacrifice is only allowed to be offered to Hashem when we have the *Beis HaMikdash*. And chickens are never used for sacrifices.

הַדְלָקַת נֵרוֹת יוֹם כִּיפּוּר / Yom Kippur Candle Lighting

The candles are lit before sunset. After lighting the candles, cover your eyes and say the following blessing:

Blessed are You, Hashem, our God, King of the universe, Who has made us holy with His mitzvos, and commanded us to light the Yom Kippur candle.

בָּרוּךְ אַתָּה יהוה אֱלֹהֵינוּ מֶלֶךְ הָעוֹלָם, אֲשֶׁר קִדְּשָׁנוּ בְּמִצְוֹתָיו, וְצִוָּנוּ לְהַדְלִיק נֵר שֶׁל יוֹם הַכִּפּוּרִים.

When Yom Kippur comes out on Shabbos we say this blessing instead.

Blessed are You, Hashem, our God, King of the universe, Who has made us holy with His mitzvos, and commanded us to light the Shabbos candle and the Yom Kippur candle.

בָּרוּךְ אַתָּה יהוה אֱלֹהֵינוּ מֶלֶךְ הָעוֹלָם, אֲשֶׁר קִדְּשָׁנוּ בְּמִצְוֹתָיו, וְצִוָּנוּ לְהַדְלִיק נֵר שֶׁל שַׁבָּת וְשֶׁל יוֹם הַכִּפּוּרִים.

On all days say:

Blessed are You, Hashem, our God, King of the universe, for keeping us alive, taking care of us, and bringing us to this time.

בָּרוּךְ אַתָּה יהוה אֱלֹהֵינוּ מֶלֶךְ הָעוֹלָם, שֶׁהֶחֱיָנוּ וְקִיְּמָנוּ וְהִגִּיעָנוּ לַזְּמַן הַזֶּה.

A Closer Look

In addition to the regular Yom Kippur candles, a special candle is lit on Erev Yom Kippur for every married man. It is called the נֵר הַבָּרִיא, Light of the Healthy. It is meant as a sign that we should have a healthy year.

Also on Yom Kippur, someone whose parent passed away lights a special candle called נֵר נְשָׁמָה, Light of the Soul. This helps them in Heaven. This candle is also called the *Yizkor* Light.

These candles stay lit the entire Yom Kippur.

No blessing is said over any of these two candles.

Did You Know??

The prophet Yeshayahu teaches us that we must observe Shabbos with joy. To increase our joy, our Sages taught us to light candles on Shabbos and *Yamim Tovim*, including Yom Kippur.

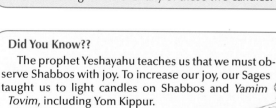

57

בְּרְכַּת הַבָּנִים / *Bircas Habanim*

There is a very beautiful custom for parents to bless their children before going to shul on Erev Yom Kippur.

Both hands are placed upon the child's head as the following blessing is said:

For a boy:

יְשִׂמְךָ אֱלֹהִים כְּאֶפְרַיִם וְכִמְנַשֶּׁה.

May Hashem make you just like Ephraim and Menashe [the grandchildren of Yaakov Avinu].

For a girl:

יְשִׂמֵךְ אֱלֹהִים כְּשָׂרָה רִבְקָה רָחֵל וְלֵאָה.

May Hashem make you just like Sarah, Rivkah, Rachel, and Leah [the four mothers of the Jewish people].

For both:

יְבָרֶכְךָ יהוה וְיִשְׁמְרֶךָ. יָאֵר יהוה פָּנָיו אֵלֶיךָ וִיחֻנֶּךָּ. יִשָּׂא יהוה פָּנָיו אֵלֶיךָ, וְיָשֵׂם לְךָ שָׁלוֹם.

May Hashem bless you and watch over you. May the light of His Face shine upon you. May Hashem look favorably on you, and bring you peace.

וִיהִי רָצוֹן מִלִּפְנֵי אָבִינוּ שֶׁבַּשָּׁמַיִם, שֶׁיִּתֵּן בְּלִבְּךָ אַהֲבָתוֹ וְיִרְאָתוֹ. וְתִהְיֶה יִרְאַת יהוה עַל פָּנֶיךָ כָּל יָמֶיךָ, שֶׁלֹּא תֶחֱטָא. וִיהִי חֶשְׁקְךָ בַּתּוֹרָה וּבַמִּצְוֹת. עֵינֶיךָ לְנֹכַח יַבִּיטוּ; פִּיךָ יְדַבֵּר חָכְמוֹת; וְלִבְּךָ יֶהְגֶּה אֵימוֹת; יָדֶיךָ יַעַסְקוּ בְּמִצְוֹת; רַגְלֶיךָ יָרוּצוּ לַעֲשׂוֹת רְצוֹן אָבִיךָ שֶׁבַּשָּׁמַיִם. יִתֵּן לְךָ בָּנִים וּבָנוֹת, צַדִּיקִים וְצִדְקָנִיּוֹת, עוֹסְקִים בַּתּוֹרָה וּבַמִּצְוֹת כָּל יְמֵיהֶם. וִיהִי מְקוֹרְךָ בָּרוּךְ. וְיַזְמִין לְךָ פַּרְנָסָתְךָ בְּהֶתֵּר, בְּנַחַת וּבְרֶוַח, מִתַּחַת יָדוֹ הָרְחָבָה, וְלֹא עַל יְדֵי מַתְּנַת בָּשָׂר וָדָם; פַּרְנָסָה שֶׁתִּהְיֶה פָנוּי לַעֲבוֹדַת יהוה. וְתִכָּתֵב וְתֵחָתֵם לְחַיִּים טוֹבִים וַאֲרֻכִּים, בְּתוֹךְ כָּל צַדִּיקֵי יִשְׂרָאֵל. אָמֵן.

May it be Hashem's desire to place His love and awe into your heart. May you fear Hashem as long as you live so that you will not sin. May you want to learn Torah and do mitzvos. May your eyes look for truth, may your mouth speak wisely, may your heart be filled with wonder and fear. May your hands always do mitzvos, and may your feet run to do whatever Hashem wants. May you have holy sons and daughters who learn Torah and do mitzvos all their lives. May Hashem let you make an honest and comfortable living, from His generous Hand, so that you will not have to take gifts and charity from other people — this way you will be able to serve Him properly. And may you be written and sealed for a good, long, life, together with all the righteous people of Israel.

A Closer Look
Our Sages teach us that there is a special kindness and forgiveness flowing from Hashem as Yom Kippur begins. That is why it is a particularly good time for parents to bless their children. Sometimes, parents add their own special blessings at the end of the prayer.

58

Did You Know??
Some parents bless their children every Friday night after shul. Even more people bless their children before Yom Kippur.

כָּל נִדְרֵי / *Kol Nidrei*

At least two Torah Scrolls are removed from the Aron Kodesh. These Scrolls are carried around the shul
so that everyone can kiss the Torah. All but two Scrolls are then put back into the *Aron Kodesh*.
Two men stand next to the *chazzan*, one on each side, holding these Scrolls.

The *chazzan* says the following verse several times and the congregation repeats it.

אוֹר זָרֻעַ לַצַּדִּיק, וּלְיִשְׁרֵי לֵב שִׂמְחָה.

Light is planted for the righteous people, and for the people who are pure in their hearts — happiness.

The *chazzan* then says this three times:

עַל דַּעַת הַמָּקוֹם וְעַל דַּעַת הַקָּהָל, בִּישִׁיבָה שֶׁל מַעְלָה, וּבִישִׁיבָה שֶׁל מַטָּה, אָנוּ מַתִּירִין לְהִתְפַּלֵּל עִם הָעֲבַרְיָנִים.

With Hashem's approval, and with the congregation's approval; in the Court in Heaven, and in the Court on Earth, we are giving permission to daven with sinners.

The *chazzan* recites *Kol Nidrei* three times. Each time his voice gets a little bit louder.
The congregation says it along with the *chazzan*, but quietly.

כָּל נִדְרֵי, וֶאֱסָרֵי, וּשְׁבוּעֵי, וַחֲרָמֵי, וְקוֹנָמֵי, וְקִנּוּסֵי, וְכִנּוּיֵי, דְּאִנְדַּרְנָא. וּדְאִשְׁתַּבַּעְנָא, וּדְאַחֲרִמְנָא, וּדְאָסַרְנָא עַל נַפְשָׁתָנָא. מִיּוֹם כִּפּוּרִים [some add: שֶׁעָבַר עַד יוֹם כִּפּוּרִים זֶה, וּמִיּוֹם כִּפּוּרִים] זֶה עַד יוֹם כִּפּוּרִים הַבָּא עָלֵינוּ לְטוֹבָה. בְּכֻלְּהוֹן אִחֲרַטְנָא בְהוֹן. כֻּלְּהוֹן יְהוֹן שָׁרָן, שְׁבִיקִין, שְׁבִיתִין, בְּטֵלִין וּמְבֻטָּלִין, לָא שְׁרִירִין וְלָא קַיָּמִין. נִדְרָנָא לָא נִדְרֵי, וֶאֱסָרָנָא לָא אֱסָרֵי, וּשְׁבוּעָתָנָא לָא שְׁבוּעוֹת.

All the different types of vows or restrictions that we took upon ourselves from the Yom Kippur (some add: of last year until this Yom Kippur, and) from this Yom Kippur until next Yom Kippur, are hereby canceled and have no power. Our vows shall not be considered vows, our restrictions shall not be considered restrictions, and our oaths shall not be considered oaths.

A Closer Look

As the *chazzan* sings Kol Nidrei, you hear its ancient, haunting melody. You can feel it enter deep into your soul, bringing you closer to doing *teshuvah*.

As we begin Yom Kippur, one would think that our first prayer would be begging Hashem for forgiveness from our sins. Why then is *Kol Nidrei* simply a statement freeing us from any vows we made?

This makes us realize the importance of each word we say. We begin Yom Kippur realizing that before we can ask Hashem to forgive us for our sins, we must first make sure we kept the promises we made.

A Closer Look

Even if we are sinners, we are allowed to daven with the rest of the congregation. Also, we should try to include any sinners in the davening and bring them closer to Hashem.

Did You Know??

The *chazzan* stands on the *bimah* with two men at his sides, holding Torah Scrolls. One reason is that when Moshe stood on a mountain praying to Hashem to save the Jewish People from the attacking Amaleikim in the desert, Aharon and Chur stood next to him.

May the entire nation of Israel, and also those who have joined the Jewish people, be forgiven for their sins, for it is as if they have been committed unintentionally.

וְנִסְלַח לְכָל עֲדַת בְּנֵי יִשְׂרָאֵל וְלַגֵּר הַגָּר בְּתוֹכָם, כִּי לְכָל הָעָם בִּשְׁגָגָה.

Please forgive the sins of the Jewish people, because You are filled with kindness, and like You have forgiven Your people from the time they were taken out of Egypt until today.

And there (after they left Egypt and sinned) it says:

סְלַח נָא לַעֲוֹן הָעָם הַזֶּה כְּגֹדֶל חַסְדֶּךָ, וְכַאֲשֶׁר נָשָׂאתָה לָעָם הַזֶּה מִמִּצְרַיִם וְעַד הֵנָּה, וְשָׁם נֶאֱמַר:

Congregation says three times, then the chazzan *says three times:*

And Hashem said, "I have forgiven just as you have said."

וַיֹּאמֶר יהוה סָלַחְתִּי כִּדְבָרֶךָ.

The chazzan *says the following* berachah *out loud, and we say it quietly with the* chazzan.
We finish it a little before the chazzan *finishes so we can answer* Amen.
Those who said the berachah *when they lit candles at home do not say it now.*

Blessed are You, Hashem, our God, King of the universe, for keeping us alive, taking care of us, and bringing us to this time.

בָּרוּךְ אַתָּה יהוה אֱלֹהֵינוּ מֶלֶךְ הָעוֹלָם, שֶׁהֶחֱיָנוּ וְקִיְּמָנוּ וְהִגִּיעָנוּ לַזְּמַן הַזֶּה.

Congregation answers:

Amen.

אָמֵן.

Did You Know??

After the Jews left Egypt, Moshe sent spies to scout out the Land of Israel. They came back with a very bad report, telling the people that giants live there, and the Jewish people will never be able to conquer the land. The people believed them and thought that Hashem was not strong enough to defeat the Canaanites. Hashem became very angry at the Jews and at the spies. Moshe prayed, begging Hashem to forgive the people. The verse, "And Hashem said, 'I have forgiven just as you have said,'" was Hashem's answer to Moshe.

Did You Know??

When men come to the synagogue for *Kol Nidrei*, they put on their *kittel* and *tallis*. This shows us that on Yom Kippur the Jewish people are like pure, white angels, who are free of any sin.

Also, the *kittel* reminds us that one day we will all pass away. People are buried in a *kittel-*like garment after they die. When we think about that, we realize we should do *teshuvah*.

A Closer Look

We ask Hashem's forgiveness for any sins we may have done, and pray that we will never do these sins again.

שְׁמַע יִשְׂרָאֵל / Shema Yisrael

אֵל מֶלֶךְ נֶאֱמָן.

God, trustworthy King.

Cover your eyes with your right hand and say this verse out loud

שְׁמַע יִשְׂרָאֵל, יהוה אֱלֹהֵינוּ, יהוה אֶחָד:

Hear, O Israel, Hashem is our God, Hashem is the only One.

On Yom Kippur, this second verse is recited out loud also.

בָּרוּךְ שֵׁם כְּבוֹד מַלְכוּתוֹ לְעוֹלָם וָעֶד.

Blessed is the Name of His wonderful kingdom forever and ever.

A Closer Look

The entire year this second verse is said quietly. Why is it said aloud only on Yom Kippur? Moshe heard this prayer from the angels in heaven when he was receiving the Torah from Hashem. The whole year we are full of sin, and do not dare say this prayer of the angels out loud. But on Yom Kippur, we raise ourselves to the level of the angels, and so we say this verse aloud, the way the angels do.

וִדּוּי / Viduy

When saying *Viduy*, we should stand without leaning, but with our head and body slightly bent.
This shows our humility and humbleness before Hashem.

Our God, and the God of our fathers, let our prayers come directly to You. Do not ignore our requests. We are not so disrespectful and stubborn to say to You, Hashem, "We are *tzaddikim*, and we have not sinned." We admit that we and our fathers have sinned.

אֱלֹהֵינוּ וֵאלֹהֵי אֲבוֹתֵינוּ, תָּבֹא לְפָנֶיךָ תְּפִלָּתֵנוּ, וְאַל תִּתְעַלַּם מִתְּחִנָּתֵנוּ, שֶׁאֵין אֲנוּ עַזֵּי פָנִים וּקְשֵׁי עֹרֶף, לוֹמַר לְפָנֶיךָ, יְהֹוָה אֱלֹהֵינוּ וֵאלֹהֵי אֲבוֹתֵינוּ, צַדִּיקִים אֲנַחְנוּ וְלֹא חָטָאנוּ, אֲבָל אֲנַחְנוּ וַאֲבוֹתֵינוּ חָטָאנוּ.

When we mention each of the following sins, we softly hit the left side of our chest
— where our heart is — with our right fist.

אָשַׁמְנוּ,

We are guilty,
and have sinned against You, Hashem.

בָּגַדְנוּ,

We have betrayed Hashem,
by not following His mitzvos.

גָּזַלְנוּ,

We have robbed
from other people.

דִּבַּרְנוּ דֹפִי.

We have told lies,
and said things to harm others.

הֶעֱוִינוּ,

We have made other people sin,
by getting them not to follow Hashem's way.

וְהִרְשַׁעְנוּ,

We have made other people do wicked things,
and caused them to sin.

זַדְנוּ,

We have sinned on purpose,
and then we tried to show that it wasn't really a sin.

חָמַסְנוּ,

We have taken from other people,
and we have taken advantage of the poor and the weak.

טָפַלְנוּ שֶׁקֶר.

We have accused other people wrongly,
by saying bad things about others.

יָעַצְנוּ רָע,

We have given bad advice,
by advising others to make the wrong choice.

כִּזַּבְנוּ,

We have misled other people,
by not keeping our word.

לַצְנוּ,

We have made fun of other people and things,
and made jokes about serious matters.

מָרַדְנוּ,

We have rebelled,
against Hashem, and showed that we don't listen to what He says.

נִאַצְנוּ,

We angered Hashem
by being disrespectful to Him.

סָרַרְנוּ,

We have turned away from Hashem,
and not done the mitzvos we should have.

A Closer Look

The *Viduy* prayers (עַל חֵטְא and אָשַׁמְנוּ) are both arranged in the order of the alphabet. This is because Hashem wrote the Torah using the 22 letters of the *aleph-beis*. We therefore remember all our sins with these same 22 letters. Also, the person who sins is destroying the world which Hashem created using these 22 letters.

Did You Know??

Viduy means *confession*, admitting we did wrong. We confess to Hashem for all sins; some that were done on purpose, and some that were done by accident.

A Closer Look

Hashem gives us all free will, the choice to choose between good and evil. It is up to us to make the correct choice and choose good.

A Closer Look

One year, on Rosh Chodesh Elul, a non-Jewish shoemaker asked the holy R' Levi Yitzchak of Berditchev, "Do you have anything to fix?"

R' Levi Yitzchak began to cry bitterly. "Rosh Hashanah is almost here and I have still not been able to fix myself!" he sobbed.

עָוִינוּ,

We have not been honest,
and convinced ourselves that we were doing the right thing.

פָּשַׁעְנוּ,

We have sinned by refusing to do certain mitzvos,
showing that we do not fully believe in Your holy Torah.

צָרַרְנוּ,

We have caused other people to suffer,
and not thought about their feelings and how we hurt them.

קִשִּׁינוּ עֹרֶף.

We have been stubborn,
and did not change our bad ways, even when You punished us.

רָשַׁעְנוּ,

We have been evil,
and not followed Your Torah.

שִׁחַתְנוּ,

We have ruined ourselves,
and acted badly in ways that changed our nature.

תִּעַבְנוּ,

We have been disgusting,
to You because of our sins.

תָּעִינוּ,

We have gone away from Your path,
instead of coming close to You.

תִּעְתָּעְנוּ.

You have let us go away from Your path,
You gave us the freedom to choose between right and wrong.
Sometimes we chose to do what is wrong.

We have turned away from You, and Your mitzvos, and from Your beautiful laws, but it was all for nothing and no good came of it.

You are fair in everything that happens to us, because You have acted with truth, and we have done evil.

What can we say to You, You, Who are in Heaven, What can we tell You, You, Who are up High, Everything that is hidden and not hidden, You know.

סַרְנוּ מִמִּצְוֹתֶיךָ וּמִמִּשְׁפָּטֶיךָ הַטּוֹבִים, וְלֹא שָׁוָה לָנוּ.

וְאַתָּה צַדִּיק עַל כָּל הַבָּא עָלֵינוּ, כִּי אֱמֶת עָשִׂיתָ וַאֲנַחְנוּ הִרְשָׁעְנוּ.

מַה נֹּאמַר לְפָנֶיךָ יוֹשֵׁב מָרוֹם, וּמַה נְּסַפֵּר לְפָנֶיךָ שׁוֹכֵן שְׁחָקִים, הֲלֹא כָּל הַנִּסְתָּרוֹת וְהַנִּגְלוֹת אַתָּה יוֹדֵעַ.

עַל חֵטְא / *Al Cheit*

When saying "*Al Cheit*," we should stand with our head and body slightly bent.
When we say the word "cheit" we softly hit the left side of our chest (where our heart is) with our right fist.
This is because the heart's desires are the source of all sins.

אַתָּה יוֹדֵעַ רָזֵי עוֹלָם, וְתַעֲלוּמוֹת סִתְרֵי כָל חָי אַתָּה חֹפֵשׂ כָּל חַדְרֵי בֶטֶן, וּבֹחֵן כְּלָיוֹת וָלֵב. אֵין דָּבָר נֶעְלָם מִמֶּךָּ, וְאֵין נִסְתָּר מִנֶּגֶד עֵינֶיךָ.

You know the secrets of the universe, all the hidden mysteries, of all living things. You search in all the hidden places, studying our thoughts and feelings. Nothing is hidden from You, Nothing is unseen from Your Eyes.

וּבְכֵן יְהִי רָצוֹן מִלְּפָנֶיךָ, יהוה אֱלֹהֵינוּ וֵאלֹהֵי אֲבוֹתֵינוּ, שֶׁתִּסְלַח לָנוּ עַל כָּל חַטֹּאתֵינוּ, וְתִמְחָל לָנוּ עַל כָּל עֲוֹנוֹתֵינוּ, וּתְכַפֶּר לָנוּ עַל כָּל פְּשָׁעֵינוּ.

And so, may You choose to forgive us for all our mistakes, excuse us for all our sins that we did on purpose, atone for us for all our sins that we did rebelliously against You.

We now go through a long list of sins. Some we have done, and some we have not — but every Jew is responsible for every other Jew, and we ask forgiveness for our own sins, and for the sins of all the Jewish people.

עַל חֵטְא שֶׁחָטָאנוּ לְפָנֶיךָ בְּאֹנֶס וּבְרָצוֹן,

For the sin we have committed in front of You even if we were forced to do it,

We said we were forced, but we really should not have done it.

וְעַל חֵטְא שֶׁחָטָאנוּ לְפָנֶיךָ בְּאִמּוּץ הַלֵּב.

For the sin we have committed in front of You because our heart was hardened,

We were stubborn and would not admit we were wrong.

עַל חֵטְא שֶׁחָטָאנוּ לְפָנֶיךָ בִּבְלִי דָעַת,

For the sin we have committed in front of You because we did not know better,

We should have studied and known better.

וְעַל חֵטְא שֶׁחָטָאנוּ לְפָנֶיךָ בְּבִטוּי שְׂפָתָיִם.

For the sin we have committed in front of You in speaking,

We should be more careful with what comes out of our mouth.

עַל חֵטְא שֶׁחָטָאנוּ לְפָנֶיךָ בְּגָלוּי וּבַסָּתֶר,

For the sin we have committed in front of You both in front of people and not in front of people,

You, Hashem, see all our sins and everything we do.

וְעַל חֵטְא שֶׁחָטָאנוּ לְפָנֶיךָ בְּגִלּוּי עֲרָיוֹת.

For the sin we have committed in front of You by doing immoral things,

Watching or doing the wrong things.

For the sin we have committed in front of You through speech,

עַל חֵטְא שֶׁחָטָאנוּ לְפָנֶיךָ בְּדִבּוּר פֶּה,

By saying the wrong things, and not thinking before we speak.

For the sin we have committed in front of You knowing and tricking,

וְעַל חֵטְא שֶׁחָטָאנוּ לְפָנֶיךָ בְּדַעַת וּבְמִרְמָה.

We used our knowledge to trick or mislead others.

For the sin we have committed in front of You by thinking the wrong thing,

עַל חֵטְא שֶׁחָטָאנוּ לְפָנֶיךָ בְּהַרְהוֹר הַלֵּב,

We thought about sins we wanted to commit.

For the sin we have committed in front of You by doing wrong to our friend,

וְעַל חֵטְא שֶׁחָטָאנוּ לְפָנֶיךָ בְּהוֹנָאַת רֵעַ.

Our friends trusted us, but we fooled them and did wrong to them.

For the sin we have committed in front of You by admitting our sin without really being sincere,

עַל חֵטְא שֶׁחָטָאנוּ לְפָנֶיךָ בְּוִדּוּי פֶּה,

We weren't really serious about doing teshuvah.

For the sin we have committed in front of You by acting wrongly,

וְעַל חֵטְא שֶׁחָטָאנוּ לְפָנֶיךָ בְּוְעִידַת זְנוּת.

By being with people and going to places where people act improperly.

For the sin we have committed in front of You on purpose and carelessly,

עַל חֵטְא שֶׁחָטָאנוּ לְפָנֶיךָ בְּזָדוֹן וּבִשְׁגָגָה,

We must do teshuvah for not being careful.

For the sin we have committed in front of You by not showing respect to parents and teachers,

וְעַל חֵטְא שֶׁחָטָאנוּ לְפָנֶיךָ בְּזִלְזוּל הוֹרִים וּמוֹרִים.

Parents bring us into this world, and our Torah teachers bring us into the World to Come.

For the sin we have committed in front of You by the wrong use of power,

עַל חֵטְא שֶׁחָטָאנוּ לְפָנֶיךָ בְּחֹזֶק יָד,

We took advantage of weak people.

For the sin we have committed in front of You by desecrating Your Name,

וְעַל חֵטְא שֶׁחָטָאנוּ לְפָנֶיךָ בְּחִלּוּל הַשֵּׁם.

People judge Judaism by the way Jews act.
If we do wrong, people will think that Judaism is bad.

For the sin we have committed in front of You by saying silly things,

עַל חֵטְא שֶׁחָטָאנוּ לְפָנֶיךָ בְּטִפְּשׁוּת פֶּה,

Our teeth are there to guard our tongue from saying something bad, and our lips guard our mouth. We have to make sure we don't say the wrong and foolish things.

For the sin we have committed in front of You by saying disgusting things,

וְעַל חֵטְא שֶׁחָטָאנוּ לְפָנֶיךָ בְּטֻמְאַת שְׂפָתָיִם.

We must always be pure, say pure things, and keep our self-respect.

For the sin we have committed in front of You by listening to the *yetzer hara* (evil inclination),

עַל חֵטְא שֶׁחָטָאנוּ לְפָנֶיךָ בְּיֵצֶר הָרָע,

Instead of fighting the yetzer hara, we sometimes encouraged him to to lead us to do bad

For the sin we have committed in front of You by doing wrong to those who know and to those who don't know,

וְעַל חֵטְא שֶׁחָטָאנוּ לְפָנֶיךָ בְּיוֹדְעִים וּבְלֹא יוֹדְעִים.

Sometimes people know we did wrong to them, sometimes they do not; but either way it is very bad.

For all these sins, God of forgiveness, please forgive us, excuse us, and atone for us.

וְעַל כֻּלָּם, אֱלוֹהַ סְלִיחוֹת, סְלַח לָנוּ, מְחַל לָנוּ, כַּפֶּר לָנוּ.

For the sin we have committed in front of You through bribery,

עַל חֵטְא שֶׁחָטָאנוּ לְפָנֶיךָ בְּכַפַּת שֹׁחַד,

We have paid someone to do wrong, or we have done wrong for payment.

For the sin we have committed in front of You by denying things and making false promises,

וְעַל חֵטְא שֶׁחָטָאנוּ לְפָנֶיךָ בְּכַחַשׁ וּבְכָזָב.

We lied about things that happened and made false promises about what we would do.

For the sin we have committed in front of You by saying *lashon hara*,

עַל חֵטְא שֶׁחָטָאנוּ לְפָנֶיךָ בְּלָשׁוֹן הָרָע,

We may not say bad things about others.

For the sin we have committed in front of You for making fun,

וְעַל חֵטְא שֶׁחָטָאנוּ לְפָנֶיךָ בְּלָצוֹן.

When someone tried to give us good advice, we mocked them.

For the sin we have committed in front of You in business dealings,

עַל חֵטְא שֶׁחָטָאנוּ לְפָנֶיךָ בְּמַשָּׂא וּבְמַתָּן,

By not dealing honestly with others.

For the sin we have committed in front of You with food and drink,

וְעַל חֵטְא שֶׁחָטָאנוּ לְפָנֶיךָ בְּמַאֲכָל וּבְמִשְׁתֶּה.

Hashem blesses us by giving us food. When we do not treat food with respect, or when we eat foods we may not eat, or eat without making a berachah, we are showing Hashem that we are not grateful for His gift.

For the sin we have committed in front of You by charging interest,

עַל חֵטְא שֶׁחָטָאנוּ לְפָנֶיךָ בְּנֶשֶׁךְ וּבְמַרְבִּית,

When we lend someone money, we are not allowed to take back more than we gave them.

For the sin we have committed in front of You by acting arrogantly,

וְעַל חֵטְא שֶׁחָטָאנוּ לְפָנֶיךָ בִּנְטִיַּת גָּרוֹן.

We act as if we are better than others.

For the sin we have committed in front of You by looking at the wrong things,

עַל חֵטְא שֶׁחָטָאנוּ לְפָנֶיךָ בְּשִׂקּוּר עָיִן,

We should not look at bad things.

For the sin we have committed in front of You by foolish, improper talk,

וְעַל חֵטְא שֶׁחָטָאנוּ לְפָנֶיךָ בְּשִׂיחַ שִׂפְתוֹתֵינוּ.

We sometimes say foolish things. Sometimes we talk without thinking. No good comes from this.

For the sin we have committed in front of You by looking down on others,

עַל חֵטְא שֶׁחָטָאנוּ לְפָנֶיךָ בְּעֵינַיִם רָמוֹת,

Hashem created us all in His image, and it is not for us to decide who is better and who is worse.

For the sin we have committed in front of You for not being ashamed,

וְעַל חֵטְא שֶׁחָטָאנוּ לְפָנֶיךָ בְּעַזּוּת מֵצַח.

If we would be embarrassed by others looking down at us for sinning, we wouldn't sin.

For all these sins, God of forgiveness, please forgive us, excuse us, and atone for us.

וְעַל כֻּלָּם, אֱלוֹהַּ סְלִיחוֹת, סְלַח לָנוּ, מְחַל לָנוּ, כַּפֶּר לָנוּ.

For the sin we have committed in front of You by not accepting our responsibility,

עַל חֵטְא שֶׁחָטָאנוּ לְפָנֶיךָ בִּפְרִיקַת עֹל,

At Har Sinai the Jewish people agreed to follow Hashem's commandments.

For the sin we have committed in front of You in matters of judgment,

וְעַל חֵטְא שֶׁחָטָאנוּ לְפָנֶיךָ בִּפְלִילוּת.

We have judged people wrongly; and even "judged" Hashem and found him "wrong" for not doing everything we want.

For the sin we have committed in front of You by taking advantage of a neighbor,

עַל חֵטְא שֶׁחָטָאנוּ לְפָנֶיךָ בִּצְדִיַּת רֵעַ,

Sometimes we take advantage of our friends. Sometimes we hurt the ones who trust us.

For the sin we have committed in front of You by being jealous,

וְעַל חֵטְא שֶׁחָטָאנוּ לְפָנֶיךָ בְּצָרוּת עָיִן.

Everything we have is a gift from Hashem. Nothing is really ours, and nothing really belongs to our friends, so there is never a reason to be jealous or not to share.

For the sin we have committed in front of You by acting improperly,

עַל חֵטְא שֶׁחָטָאנוּ לְפָנֶיךָ בְּקַלּוּת רֹאשׁ,

Every person has responsibilities that must be taken seriously.

For the sin we have committed in front of You by being stubborn,

וְעַל חֵטְא שֶׁחָטָאנוּ לְפָנֶיךָ בְּקַשְׁיוּת עֹרֶף.

Hashem often punishes us to make us improve. We are sometimes stubborn and refuse to get the message.

For the sin we have committed in front of You by running to do evil,

עַל חֵטְא שֶׁחָטָאנוּ לְפָנֶיךָ בְּרִיצַת רַגְלַיִם לְהָרַע,

We make our sinning even worse when we love the sin so much that we run to do it.

For the sin we have committed in front of You by gossiping,

וְעַל חֵטְא שֶׁחָטָאנוּ לְפָנֶיךָ בִּרְכִילוּת.

Telling someone about what others did to him is a sin — it is a sin to say it and a sin to listen.

A Closer Look

When we sin, we are affecting all other people. This can be compared to a group of people in a boat at sea. One person begins to drill a hole under his own seat.

"Stop, stop!" everyone yells. "You will kill us all!"

The person simply stares at everyone and says, "Why are you bothering me? I'm only drilling a hole under my seat, not under yours." He does not realize that his actions will cause the entire boat to sink.

For the sin we have committed in front of You by swearing falsely or for no reason,

עַל חֵטְא שֶׁחָטָאנוּ לְפָנֶיךָ בִּשְׁבוּעַת שָׁוְא,

When we swear we use Hashem's Name. It is a big sin to take an oath improperly,

For the sin we have committed in front of You by hating other people,

וְעַל חֵטְא שֶׁחָטָאנוּ לְפָנֶיךָ בְּשִׂנְאַת חִנָּם.

Every person is created by Hashem in His image.
One can be unhappy with what another person does, but not with the other person himself.

For the sin we have committed in front of You by not helping others,

עַל חֵטְא שֶׁחָטָאנוּ לְפָנֶיךָ בִּתְשׂוּמֶת יָד,

How can we expect Hashem to help us, if we are not willing to help others?

For the sin we have committed in front of You by being confused,

וְעַל חֵטְא שֶׁחָטָאנוּ לְפָנֶיךָ בְּתִמְהוֹן לֵבָב.

We must remember that everything that happens to us comes from Hashem,
Who is kind, loving, and fair.

For all these sins, God of forgiveness, please forgive us, excuse us, and atone for us.

וְעַל כֻּלָּם, אֱלוֹהַּ סְלִיחוֹת, סְלַח לָנוּ, מְחַל לָנוּ, כַּפֶּר לָנוּ.

This ends the alphabetical listing of our personal sins.
Next we list groups of sins based on their punishments. We begin with the mildest (bringing an animal sacrifice),
and end with the most severe (the death penalty). Just reminding ourselves of these punishments helps us
have a more sincere repentance, which will make the punishments unnecessary.

And for the sins which require us to bring an *olah* sacrifice,

וְעַל חֲטָאִים שֶׁאָנוּ חַיָּבִים עֲלֵיהֶם עוֹלָה.

This is how to do teshuvah for not fulfilling a positive commandment
(such as not eating matzoh on Pesach) or of thinking bad things.

And for the sins which require us to bring a *chatas* sacrifice,

וְעַל חֲטָאִים שֶׁאָנוּ חַיָּבִים עֲלֵיהֶם חַטָּאת.

This is a sin offering which we bring for breaking certain commandments carelessly
(such as doing work on Shabbos, or eating chametz on Pesach).

A Closer Look

The best way for us to learn about asking forgiveness is to first learn how to forgive others. We can't expect Hashem to forgive us if we don't forgive others first.

In addition to learning to forgive others, we must learn to forgive ourselves. All of us make mistakes, and we must learn from them. We should never say that we are so bad that we should give up hope. We can always improve and even become *tzaddikim*.

And for the sins which require us to bring an *oleh* or *yored* offering, whose value changes based on the person's wealth,

וְעַל חֲטָאִים שֶׁאָנוּ חַיָּבִים עֲלֵיהֶם קָרְבַּן עוֹלֶה וְיוֹרֵד.

This is brought for swearing falsely in court about someone's testimony and for five other specific sins mentioned in the Torah.

And for the sins which require us to bring an "*asham*" sacrifice, for a sin we definitely did or for a sin we might have done,

וְעַל חֲטָאִים שֶׁאָנוּ חַיָּבִים עֲלֵיהֶם אָשָׁם וַדַּאי וְתָלוּי.

Certain sins require an "asham" sacrifice. There is also a special "asham" sacrifice which is brought if we are not sure if we did certain sins.

And for the sins for which we receive a beating for acting rebelliously,

וְעַל חֲטָאִים שֶׁאָנוּ חַיָּבִים עֲלֵיהֶם מַכַּת מַרְדּוּת.

This is the punishment for violating a Rabbinic decree on purpose, or to force soemone to do certain mitzvos.

And for the sins for which we receive forty lashes,

וְעַל חֲטָאִים שֶׁאָנוּ חַיָּבִים עֲלֵיהֶם מַלְקוּת אַרְבָּעִים.

This is the punishment one receives when he violates one of the Torah's negative commandments that does not have another specific punishment.

And for the sins for which we receive the death penalty from Heaven,

וְעַל חֲטָאִים שֶׁאָנוּ חַיָּבִים עֲלֵיהֶם מִיתָה בִּידֵי שָׁמָיִם.

This punishment means that a person does not live as long as he was supposed to.

And for the sins for which we receive *kareis* and childlessness,

וְעַל חֲטָאִים שֶׁאָנוּ חַיָּבִים עֲלֵיהֶם כָּרֵת וַעֲרִירִי.

This punishment (kareis) means that a person's soul can be cut off from the World to Come, he will die young, or he will not have children.

And for the sins for which a *beis din* will kill us by either stoning, burning, beheading, or strangling,

וְעַל חֲטָאִים שֶׁאָנוּ חַיָּבִים עֲלֵיהֶם אַרְבַּע מִיתוֹת בֵּית דִּין – סְקִילָה, שְׂרֵפָה, הֶרֶג, וְחֶנֶק.

Since the destruction of the Second Beis HaMikdash, a beis din cannot order the death penalty. Hashem, Himself, finds the proper way to punish this person.

Did You Know??
An "*oleh* or *yored*" (up or down) offering depends on how much the sinner can afford. If he is rich, he spends more. If he is poor, he spends less.

For disobeying the positive commandments,

עַל מִצְוַת עֲשֵׂה

There are 248 commandments in the Torah to do something.

And for disobeying the negative commandments,

וְעַל מִצְוַת לֹא תַעֲשֶׂה,

There are 365 negative commandments in the Torah not to do something.

Whether the sin can be fixed by now doing the right thing,

בֵּין שֶׁיֵּשׁ בָּהּ קוּם עֲשֵׂה,

Or whether it cannot be fixed by now doing the right thing,

וּבֵין שֶׁאֵין בָּהּ קוּם עֲשֵׂה.

Not every sin can be easily fixed.

Those sins that we know about, and those sins that we do not know about. Those sins that we know about, we have already admitted to You. And those sins that we do not know about, You still know about them, as it says in the Torah: The hidden sins are for Hashem to know about, but the sins that we know about are ours and our children's forever; (and we are obligated) to fulfill all the words of the Torah. For You are the One Who forgives Israel, and the One Who pardons the tribes in every generation. Besides You, we have no other king who pardons and forgives us; Only You.

אֶת הַגְּלוּיִם לָנוּ וְאֶת שֶׁאֵינָם גְּלוּיִם לָנוּ, אֶת הַגְּלוּיִם לָנוּ, כְּבָר אֲמַרְנוּם לְפָנֶיךָ, וְהוֹדִינוּ לְךָ עֲלֵיהֶם, וְאֶת שֶׁאֵינָם גְּלוּיִם לָנוּ, לְפָנֶיךָ הֵם גְּלוּיִם וִידוּעִים, כַּדָּבָר שֶׁנֶּאֱמַר, הַנִּסְתָּרֹת לַיהוה אֱלֹהֵינוּ, וְהַנִּגְלֹת לָנוּ וּלְבָנֵינוּ עַד עוֹלָם, לַעֲשׂוֹת אֶת כָּל דִּבְרֵי הַתּוֹרָה הַזֹּאת. כִּי אַתָּה סָלְחָן לְיִשְׂרָאֵל וּמָחֳלָן לְשִׁבְטֵי יְשֻׁרוּן בְּכָל דּוֹר וָדוֹר, וּמִבַּלְעָדֶיךָ אֵין לָנוּ מֶלֶךְ מוֹחֵל וְסוֹלֵחַ אֶלָּא אָתָּה.

We now finish the Viduy prayer by begging Hashem for mercy since we are small and weak. We pray that Hashem will forgive us and not punish us.

My God, before I was born, I was not worth anything. But now that I have been born, I am so unworthy that it is as if I have not been born.

My whole life, I am just dust, even moreso after I die. In front of You I am like a vessel filled with shame and embarrassment.

May it be Your Will, Hashem, our God, and the God of our fathers, that I will not sin anymore. And all that I have sinned, will You please wash me clean with Your great mercy, but not by punishing me or making me suffer by being sick.

אֱלֹהַי, עַד שֶׁלֹּא נוֹצַרְתִּי אֵינִי כְדַאי, וְעַכְשָׁו שֶׁנּוֹצַרְתִּי כְּאִלּוּ לֹא נוֹצַרְתִּי, עָפָר אֲנִי בְּחַיַּי, קַל וָחֹמֶר בְּמִיתָתִי. הֲרֵי אֲנִי לְפָנֶיךָ כִּכְלִי מָלֵא בוּשָׁה וּכְלִמָּה. יְהִי רָצוֹן מִלְּפָנֶיךָ, יהוה אֱלֹהַי וֵאלֹהֵי אֲבוֹתַי, שֶׁלֹּא אֶחֱטָא עוֹד, וּמַה שֶּׁחָטָאתִי לְפָנֶיךָ מָרֵק בְּרַחֲמֶיךָ הָרַבִּים, אֲבָל לֹא עַל יְדֵי יִסּוּרִים וָחֳלָיִם רָעִים.

י"ג מִדּוֹת / Yud Gimmel Middos

We now say *Selichos*, asking Hashem to forgive us for every sin we have done.
We have already been saying *Selichos* (Prayers of Forgiveness) since before Rosh Hashanah.

And Hashem passed before him (Moshe) and said:

וַיַּעֲבֹר יהוה עַל פָּנָיו וַיִּקְרָא:

Hashem, Hashem, God, Compassionate and Graceful, Slow to anger, and full of Kindness and Truth, Who holds on to kindness for thousands of generations, Who forgives sins, sins that we did on purpose and by mistake, and Who cleanses us.

יהוה, יהוה, אֵל, רַחוּם, וְחַנּוּן, אֶרֶךְ אַפַּיִם, וְרַב חֶסֶד, וֶאֱמֶת, נֹצֵר חֶסֶד לָאֲלָפִים, נֹשֵׂא עָוֹן, וָפֶשַׁע, וְחַטָּאָה, וְנַקֵּה.

May You forgive our sins and mistakes and make us Your people. Forgive us, our Father, for we have made mistakes. Pardon us, our King, for we have even sinned on purpose. You, Hashem, are good and forgive. You are very kind to everyone who calls out to You.

וְסָלַחְתָּ לַעֲוֹנֵנוּ וּלְחַטָּאתֵנוּ וּנְחַלְתָּנוּ. סְלַח לָנוּ אָבִינוּ כִּי חָטָאנוּ, מְחַל לָנוּ מַלְכֵּנוּ כִּי פָשָׁעְנוּ. כִּי אַתָּה אֲדֹנָי טוֹב וְסַלָּח, וְרַב חֶסֶד לְכָל קֹרְאֶיךָ.

Did You Know??
A main part of our *Selichos* is the *Yud Gimmel Middos* (The Thirteen Attributes of Mercy) that list Hashem's qualities of mercy and forgiveness.

Did You Know??
Hashem gives reward for 2,000 generations but punishes for only four generations. Hashem's kindness is 500 times as great as His punishment!

A Closer Look
This prayer appears in the Torah after the Children of Israel sinned by worshiping the Golden Calf in the desert, after leaving Egypt. In His anger, Hashem considers destroying all of the Jewish People. They have just seen His great miracles, and already they are worshiping an idol! But then He appears to Moshe with a vision of someone dressed as a *chazzan*, wrapped in a *tallis*. Hashem then taught Moshe these Thirteen Attributes. He explained to Moshe that whenever the Jewish People sin, they should recite this prayer in this order, and He will forgive them.

We learn from this that no matter what we do, as long as we do proper *teshuvah*, and commit never to do it again, we can be forgiven.

שְׁמַע קוֹלֵנוּ / Shema Koleinu

Each of the next six sentences are first said aloud by the *chazzan*
and then by the congregation (except numbers 3 and 4, which are said quietly):

1. Listen to us, Hashem, our God, have pity on us, and accept our prayer with mercy.

2. Bring us back to You, Hashem, and we shall return to You. Let us be as we used to be.

The next two sentences are said quietly:

3. Listen to what we say, and understand what we are thinking.

4. May what we say and what we think find favor with You, Hashem, our Rock and Redeemer.

5. Do not throw us away from You, and don't take Your Holiness away from us.

6. Do not send us away when we are old. Do not abandon us when we have no strength.

Do not leave us, Hashem, our God, do not be far away from us.

Show us a good sign, so that our enemies will see it, and be embarrassed. You, Hashem, will help us and comfort us. We have trusted in You, Hashem, and You will answer us.

שְׁמַע קוֹלֵנוּ יהוה אֱלֹהֵינוּ, חוּס וְרַחֵם עָלֵינוּ, וְקַבֵּל בְּרַחֲמִים וּבְרָצוֹן אֶת תְּפִלָּתֵנוּ.

הֲשִׁיבֵנוּ יהוה אֵלֶיךָ וְנָשׁוּבָה, חַדֵּשׁ יָמֵינוּ כְּקֶדֶם.

אֲמָרֵינוּ הַאֲזִינָה יהוה, בִּינָה הֲגִיגֵנוּ.

יִהְיוּ לְרָצוֹן אִמְרֵי פִינוּ וְהֶגְיוֹן לִבֵּנוּ לְפָנֶיךָ, יהוה צוּרֵנוּ וְגֹאֲלֵנוּ.

אַל תַּשְׁלִיכֵנוּ מִלְּפָנֶיךָ, וְרוּחַ קָדְשְׁךָ אַל תִּקַּח מִמֶּנּוּ.

אַל תַּשְׁלִיכֵנוּ לְעֵת זִקְנָה, כִּכְלוֹת כֹּחֵנוּ אַל תַּעַזְבֵנוּ.

אַל תַּעַזְבֵנוּ יהוה, אֱלֹהֵינוּ אַל תִּרְחַק מִמֶּנּוּ.

עֲשֵׂה עִמָּנוּ אוֹת לְטוֹבָה, וְיִרְאוּ שׂוֹנְאֵינוּ וְיֵבֹשׁוּ, כִּי אַתָּה יהוה עֲזַרְתָּנוּ וְנִחַמְתָּנוּ. כִּי לְךָ יהוה הוֹחָלְנוּ, אַתָּה תַעֲנֶה אֲדֹנָי אֱלֹהֵינוּ.

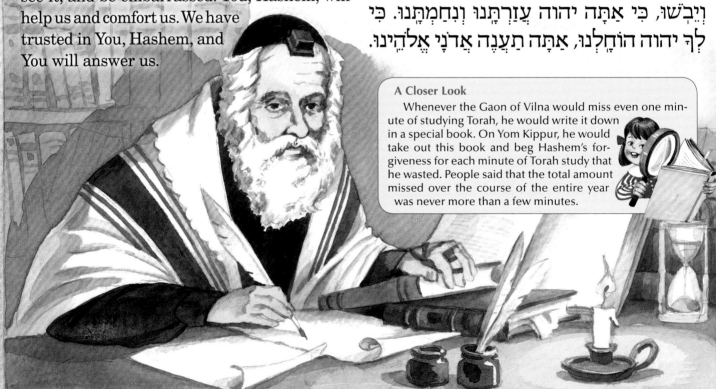

A Closer Look

Whenever the Gaon of Vilna would miss even one minute of studying Torah, he would write it down in a special book. On Yom Kippur, he would take out this book and beg Hashem's forgiveness for each minute of Torah study that he wasted. People said that the total amount missed over the course of the entire year was never more than a few minutes.

Mishnayos of Yom Kippur

This is a summary of the first chapter in Mishnah *Yoma*, the tractate that has the laws of Yom Kippur. This chapter starts teaching us about the special service of the Kohen Gadol in the *Beis HaMikdash* on Yom Kippur. Some people study this tractate on Yom Kippur.

1. Seven days before Yom Kippur, the Kohen Gadol leaves his house and moves into the Official's Chamber (the private office of the Kohen Gadol). At the same time, another Kohen is also prepared to do the Yom Kippur service, just in case anything happens to the Kohen Gadol and he is not able to do the Yom Kippur service.

2. The Kohen Gadol may do any of the services in the *Beis HaMikdash* any day he wants, but during these seven days, the Kohen Gadol must practice doing many of the services.

3. Sages from the Sanhedrin teach the Kohen Gadol all the laws about the Yom Kippur service. On the morning of the day before Yom Kippur, they show him bulls, rams, and sheep, types of animals that will be sacrificed on Yom Kippur. This is to make sure that he will know how the different animals look.

4. During those seven days the Kohen Gadol can eat as much as he wishes. But on the afternoon of Erev Yom Kippur they would not let him eat much, because the food might make him too tired.

5. The Sages from the Sanhedrin then put the Kohen Gadol under the care of the elders of the Kohanim and brought him to the chamber of Avtinas. The Sages would make the Kohen Gadol swear that he would not make any changes in the Yom Kippur service. Then the Kohen Gadol would cry, because this implied that they did not trust him. The elders would weep as well, because they had to suspect him.

6. If the Kohen Gadol was a scholar, then he would teach the laws; if he was not a scholar, then the rabbis would teach him. If he was used to reading *Tanach* by himself (from a scroll, like our Torah), he would read sections of *Tanach*; if not, then they would read to him from *Tanach*.

7. If the Kohen Gadol would begin to fall asleep, young Kohanim would snap their fingers to wake him up and tell him to put his feet on the cold stone floor to wake him up. They would make sure he stayed awake until the morning.

8. Every day at about dawn, Kohanim remove from the Altar burnt ashes from the previous day's sacrifices. On Yom Kippur, this was done earlier — any time starting from midnight (so the Kohen Gadol would be able to rest after doing it). On Pesach, Shavuos, and Succos, it was done much earlier, because many sacrifices were brought, and it took a long time to clear it all off. On those holidays, by the time morning came, the Courtyard was already filled with Jews bringing their Yom Tov sacrifices.

קְרִיאַת הַתּוֹרָה לְיוֹם הַכִּפּוּרִים
Torah Reading for Yom Kippur

The English beneath the Hebrew text is a concise adaptation of the story.

ויקרא ט"ז: א - לד

כהן - א וַיְדַבֵּ֨ר יְהֹוָ֜ה אֶל־מֹשֶׁ֗ה אַחֲרֵ֣י מ֔וֹת שְׁנֵ֖י בְּנֵ֣י אַהֲרֹ֑ן בְּקׇרְבָתָ֥ם לִפְנֵֽי־יְהֹוָ֖ה וַיָּמֻֽתוּ׃ ב וַיֹּ֨אמֶר יְהֹוָ֜ה אֶל־מֹשֶׁ֗ה דַּבֵּר֮ אֶל־אַהֲרֹ֣ן אָחִ֒יךָ֒ וְאַל־יָבֹ֤א בְכׇל־עֵת֙ אֶל־הַקֹּ֔דֶשׁ מִבֵּ֖ית לַפָּרֹ֑כֶת אֶל־פְּנֵ֨י הַכַּפֹּ֜רֶת אֲשֶׁ֤ר עַל־הָֽאָרֹן֙ וְלֹ֣א יָמ֔וּת כִּ֚י בֶּֽעָנָ֔ן אֵרָאֶ֖ה עַל־הַכַּפֹּֽרֶת׃ ג בְּזֹ֛את יָבֹ֥א אַהֲרֹ֖ן אֶל־הַקֹּ֑דֶשׁ בְּפַ֧ר בֶּן־בָּקָ֛ר לְחַטָּ֖את וְאַ֥יִל לְעֹלָֽה׃

(בשבת: לוי) - ד כְּתֹֽנֶת־בַּ֨ד קֹ֜דֶשׁ יִלְבָּ֗שׁ וּמִֽכְנְסֵי־בַד֮ יִהְי֣וּ עַל־בְּשָׂרוֹ֒ וּבְאַבְנֵ֥ט בַּד֙ יַחְגֹּ֔ר וּבְמִצְנֶ֥פֶת בַּ֖ד יִצְנֹ֑ף בִּגְדֵי־קֹ֣דֶשׁ הֵ֔ם וְרָחַ֥ץ בַּמַּ֛יִם אֶת־בְּשָׂר֖וֹ וּלְבֵשָֽׁם׃ ה וּמֵאֵ֗ת עֲדַת֙ בְּנֵ֣י יִשְׂרָאֵ֔ל יִקַּ֛ח שְׁנֵֽי־שְׂעִירֵ֥י עִזִּ֖ים לְחַטָּ֑את וְאַ֥יִל אֶחָ֖ד לְעֹלָֽה׃ ו וְהִקְרִ֧יב אַהֲרֹ֛ן אֶת־פַּ֥ר הַחַטָּ֖את אֲשֶׁר־ל֑וֹ וְכִפֶּ֥ר בַּעֲד֖וֹ וּבְעַ֥ד בֵּיתֽוֹ׃

לוי (בשבת: שלישי) - ז וְלָקַ֖ח אֶת־שְׁנֵ֣י הַשְּׂעִירִ֑ם וְהֶעֱמִ֤יד אֹתָם֙ לִפְנֵ֣י יְהֹוָ֔ה פֶּ֖תַח אֹ֥הֶל מוֹעֵֽד׃ ח וְנָתַ֧ן אַהֲרֹ֛ן עַל־שְׁנֵ֥י הַשְּׂעִירִ֖ם גֹּרָל֑וֹת גּוֹרָ֤ל אֶחָד֙ לַֽיהֹוָ֔ה וְגוֹרָ֥ל אֶחָ֖ד לַעֲזָאזֵֽל׃ ט וְהִקְרִ֤יב אַהֲרֹן֙ אֶת־הַשָּׂעִ֔יר אֲשֶׁ֨ר עָלָ֥ה עָלָ֛יו הַגּוֹרָ֖ל לַיהֹוָ֑ה וְעָשָׂ֖הוּ חַטָּֽאת׃ י וְהַשָּׂעִ֗יר אֲשֶׁר֩ עָלָ֨ה עָלָ֤יו הַגּוֹרָל֙ לַעֲזָאזֵ֔ל יׇֽעֳמַד־חַ֛י לִפְנֵ֥י יְהֹוָ֖ה לְכַפֵּ֣ר עָלָ֑יו לְשַׁלַּ֥ח אֹת֛וֹ לַעֲזָאזֵ֖ל הַמִּדְבָּֽרָה׃ יא וְהִקְרִ֨יב אַהֲרֹ֜ן אֶת־פַּ֤ר הַֽחַטָּאת֙ אֲשֶׁר־ל֔וֹ וְכִפֶּ֥ר בַּֽעֲד֖וֹ וּבְעַ֣ד בֵּית֑וֹ וְשָׁחַ֛ט אֶת־פַּ֥ר הַֽחַטָּ֖את אֲשֶׁר־לֽוֹ׃

שלישי (בשבת: רביעי) - יב וְלָקַ֣ח מְלֹֽא־הַ֠מַּחְתָּ֠ה גַּחֲלֵי־אֵ֞שׁ מֵעַ֤ל הַמִּזְבֵּ֙חַ֙ מִלִּפְנֵ֣י יְהֹוָ֔ה וּמְלֹ֣א חׇפְנָ֔יו קְטֹ֥רֶת סַמִּ֖ים דַּקָּ֑ה וְהֵבִ֖יא מִבֵּ֥ית לַפָּרֹֽכֶת׃ יג וְנָתַ֧ן אֶת־הַקְּטֹ֛רֶת עַל־הָאֵ֖שׁ לִפְנֵ֣י יְהֹוָ֑ה וְכִסָּ֣ה ׀ עֲנַ֣ן הַקְּטֹ֗רֶת אֶת־הַכַּפֹּ֛רֶת אֲשֶׁ֥ר עַל־הָעֵד֖וּת וְלֹ֥א יָמֽוּת׃ יד וְלָקַח֙ מִדַּ֣ם הַפָּ֔ר וְהִזָּ֧ה בְאֶצְבָּע֛וֹ עַל־פְּנֵ֥י הַכַּפֹּ֖רֶת קֵ֑דְמָה וְלִפְנֵ֣י הַכַּפֹּ֗רֶת יַזֶּ֧ה שֶֽׁבַע־פְּעָמִ֛ים מִן־הַדָּ֖ם בְּאֶצְבָּעֽוֹ׃ טו וְשָׁחַ֣ט אֶת־

After Aharon's two sons died, Hashem spoke to Moshe and said: Tell your brother, Aharon, about the laws of entering the Sanctuary. He is not allowed to enter the Holy of Holies whenever he wants, or he will die since I can be seen in a cloud on the Ark's cover. Aharon can only enter the Holy of Holies at a certain time, with a bull and a ram sacrifice.

He should wear a holy linen robe, linen pants, and a linen belt. His head should be covered with a linen turban — these are holy clothes. Before he puts these on, he should first bathe himself in a *mikveh*. He is to bring two male goats as a sin-offering and a ram as a burnt-offering from the people of Israel. For himself, he should bring a bull as a sin-offering so that he will be forgiven for his sins.

Aharon should then place two lots upon the two male goats. One should say "for Hashem," and the second should say, "for Azazel." The goat marked for Hashem should be sacrificed, and the other goat should be put aside.

[The Torah then teaches the details of how Aharon and future Kohanim Gedolim should bring the day's sacrifices in the Holy and the Holy of Holies.]

שְׂעִיר הַחַטָּאת אֲשֶׁר לָעָם וְהֵבִיא אֶת־דָּמוֹ אֶל־מִבֵּית לַפָּרֹכֶת וְעָשָׂה אֶת־דָּמוֹ כַּאֲשֶׁר עָשָׂה לְדַם הַפָּר וְהִזָּה אֹתוֹ עַל־הַכַּפֹּרֶת וְלִפְנֵי הַכַּפֹּרֶת: יז וְכִפֶּר עַל־הַקֹּדֶשׁ מִטֻּמְאֹת בְּנֵי יִשְׂרָאֵל וּמִפִּשְׁעֵיהֶם לְכָל־חַטֹּאתָם וְכֵן יַעֲשֶׂה לְאֹהֶל מוֹעֵד הַשֹּׁכֵן אִתָּם בְּתוֹךְ טֻמְאֹתָם: יז וְכָל־אָדָם לֹא־יִהְיֶה | בְּאֹהֶל מוֹעֵד בְּבֹאוֹ לְכַפֵּר בַּקֹּדֶשׁ עַד־צֵאתוֹ וְכִפֶּר בַּעֲדוֹ וּבְעַד בֵּיתוֹ וּבְעַד כָּל־קְהַל יִשְׂרָאֵל:

רביעי (בשבת: חמישי) - יח וְיָצָא אֶל־הַמִּזְבֵּחַ אֲשֶׁר לִפְנֵי־יהוה וְכִפֶּר עָלָיו וְלָקַח מִדַּם הַפָּר וּמִדַּם הַשָּׂעִיר וְנָתַן עַל־קַרְנוֹת הַמִּזְבֵּחַ סָבִיב: יט וְהִזָּה עָלָיו מִן־הַדָּם בְּאֶצְבָּעוֹ שֶׁבַע פְּעָמִים וְטִהֲרוֹ וְקִדְּשׁוֹ מִטֻּמְאֹת בְּנֵי

יִשְׂרָאֵל: כ וְכִלָּה מִכַּפֵּר אֶת־הַקֹּדֶשׁ וְאֶת־אֹהֶל מוֹעֵד וְאֶת־הַמִּזְבֵּחַ וְהִקְרִיב אֶת־הַשָּׂעִיר הֶחָי: כא וְסָמַךְ אַהֲרֹן אֶת־שְׁתֵּי יָדָו עַל־רֹאשׁ הַשָּׂעִיר הַחַי וְהִתְוַדָּה עָלָיו אֶת־כָּל־עֲוֺנֹת בְּנֵי יִשְׂרָאֵל וְאֶת־כָּל־פִּשְׁעֵיהֶם לְכָל־חַטֹּאתָם וְנָתַן אֹתָם עַל־רֹאשׁ הַשָּׂעִיר וְשִׁלַּח בְּיַד־אִישׁ עִתִּי הַמִּדְבָּרָה: כב וְנָשָׂא הַשָּׂעִיר עָלָיו אֶת־כָּל־עֲוֺנֹתָם אֶל־אֶרֶץ גְּזֵרָה וְשִׁלַּח אֶת־הַשָּׂעִיר בַּמִּדְבָּר: כג וּבָא אַהֲרֹן אֶל־אֹהֶל מוֹעֵד וּפָשַׁט אֶת־בִּגְדֵי הַבָּד אֲשֶׁר לָבַשׁ בְּבֹאוֹ אֶל־הַקֹּדֶשׁ וְהִנִּיחָם שָׁם: כד וְרָחַץ אֶת־בְּשָׂרוֹ בַמַּיִם בְּמָקוֹם קָדוֹשׁ וְלָבַשׁ אֶת־בְּגָדָיו וְיָצָא וְעָשָׂה אֶת־עֹלָתוֹ וְאֶת־עֹלַת הָעָם וְכִפֶּר בַּעֲדוֹ וּבְעַד הָעָם:

וְאֵת חֵלֶב הַחַטָּאת יַקְטִיר הַמִּזְבֵּחָה: כו וְהַמְשַׁלֵּחַ אֶת־הַשָּׂעִיר לַעֲזָאזֵל יְכַבֵּס בְּגָדָיו וְרָחַץ אֶת־בְּשָׂרוֹ בַּמָּיִם וְאַחֲרֵי־כֵן יָבוֹא אֶל־הַמַּחֲנֶה: כז וְאֵת פַּר הַחַטָּאת וְאֵת | שְׂעִיר הַחַטָּאת אֲשֶׁר הוּבָא אֶת־דָּמָם לְכַפֵּר בַּקֹּדֶשׁ יוֹצִיא אֶל־מִחוּץ לַמַּחֲנֶה וְשָׂרְפוּ בָאֵשׁ אֶת־עֹרֹתָם וְאֶת־בְּשָׂרָם וְאֶת־פִּרְשָׁם: כח וְהַשֹּׂרֵף אֹתָם יְכַבֵּס בְּגָדָיו וְרָחַץ אֶת־בְּשָׂרוֹ בַּמָּיִם וְאַחֲרֵי־כֵן יָבוֹא אֶל־הַמַּחֲנֶה: כט וְהָיְתָה לָכֶם לְחֻקַּת עוֹלָם בַּחֹדֶשׁ הַשְּׁבִיעִי בֶּעָשׂוֹר לַחֹדֶשׁ תְּעַנּוּ אֶת־נַפְשֹׁתֵיכֶם וְכָל־מְלָאכָה לֹא תַעֲשׂוּ הָאֶזְרָח וְהַגֵּר הַגָּר בְּתוֹכְכֶם: ל כִּי־בַיּוֹם

הַזֶּה יְכַפֵּר עֲלֵיכֶם לְטַהֵר אֶתְכֶם מִכֹּל חַטֹּאתֵיכֶם לִפְנֵי יהוה תִּטְהָרוּ: שַׁבַּת שַׁבָּתוֹן הִיא לָכֶם וְעִנִּיתֶם אֶת־נַפְשֹׁתֵיכֶם חֻקַּת עוֹלָם: לב וְכִפֶּר הַכֹּהֵן אֲשֶׁר־יִמְשַׁח אֹתוֹ וַאֲשֶׁר יְמַלֵּא אֶת־יָדוֹ לְכַהֵן תַּחַת אָבִיו וְלָבַשׁ אֶת־בִּגְדֵי הַבָּד בִּגְדֵי הַקֹּדֶשׁ: לג וְכִפֶּר אֶת־מִקְדַּשׁ הַקֹּדֶשׁ וְאֶת־אֹהֶל מוֹעֵד וְאֶת־הַמִּזְבֵּחַ יְכַפֵּר וְעַל הַכֹּהֲנִים וְעַל־כָּל־עַם הַקָּהָל יְכַפֵּר: לד וְהָיְתָה־זֹּאת לָכֶם לְחֻקַּת עוֹלָם לְכַפֵּר עַל־בְּנֵי יִשְׂרָאֵל מִכָּל־חַטֹּאתָם אַחַת בַּשָּׁנָה וַיַּעַשׂ כַּאֲשֶׁר צִוָּה יהוה אֶת־מֹשֶׁה:

When Aharon is finished with these sacrifices, he should take the goat marked "for Azazel," and place both hands upon its head. He should then confess all the sins that the Jews did and send the goat with another person into the desert. This goat will carry all the sins of the Jewish people into a desolate land.

Aharon should take off his holy linen clothing, and again bathe in the *mikveh*. He then performs other services with other sacrifices (wearing the usual garments of a Kohen Gadol).

This shall be done every year on Yom Kippur. On Yom Kippur you should neither eat nor work. This is the day that you will rid yourself of all your sins, and become pure.

Did You Know??
Aharon was the first Kohen. He was also the first Kohen Gadol (High Priest). Aharon was the first person to perform the Yom Kippur service. Only the Kohen Gadol may perform the Yom Kippur services in the *Mishkan* or the *Beis HaMikdash*.

A Closer Look
We read this portion on Yom Kippur because it explains what the Kohen Gadol does on Yom Kippur in the *Beis HaMikdash*.
Also, we see that the Torah mentions the death of Aharon's two sons on Yom Kippur. This is to teach us that just as Yom Kippur brings forgiveness to the Jewish people, the death of righteous people also brings forgiveness to the Jewish people.

עֲבוֹדָה / *Avodah*

In *Mussaf* of Yom Kippur, we describe the special Temple Service of the day. The portions here describe the Kohen Gadol's viduy, the Jews bowing, and the Kohen Gadol's sprinkling the blood. These sections are said together by the entire congregation:

וְכַךְ הָיָה אוֹמֵר: אָנָּא הַשֵּׁם, חָטָאתִי, עָוִיתִי, פָּשַׁעְתִּי לְפָנֶיךָ אֲנִי וּבֵיתִי. אָנָּא בַשֵּׁם, כַּפֶּר נָא לַחֲטָאִים וְלַעֲוֹנוֹת וְלַפְּשָׁעִים שֶׁחָטָאתִי וְשֶׁעָוִיתִי וְשֶׁפָּשַׁעְתִּי לְפָנֶיךָ אֲנִי וּבֵיתִי, כַּכָּתוּב בְּתוֹרַת מֹשֶׁה עַבְדֶּךָ, מִפִּי כְבוֹדֶךָ: כִּי בַיּוֹם הַזֶּה יְכַפֵּר עֲלֵיכֶם לְטַהֵר אֶתְכֶם, מִכֹּל חַטֹּאתֵיכֶם לִפְנֵי יהוה -

And he (the Kohen) would say, "Please Hashem, I and my family have sinned by accident and on purpose also. I beg You to forgive us. As it is written in the Torah, given straight from Your mouth to Moshe Your servant: 'Because on this day (Yom Kippur) he (the Kohen) will atone for you to cleanse you and make you pure from all your sins, in front of Hashem.'"

When we say כּוֹרְעִים, we kneel; when we say מִשְׁתַּחֲוִים we also put our face to the floor. We stay this way until the end of the paragraph.

וְהַכֹּהֲנִים וְהָעָם הָעוֹמְדִים בָּעֲזָרָה, כְּשֶׁהָיוּ שׁוֹמְעִים אֶת הַשֵּׁם הַנִּכְבָּד וְהַנּוֹרָא, מְפֹרָשׁ, יוֹצֵא מִפִּי כֹהֵן גָּדוֹל בִּקְדֻשָּׁה וּבְטָהֳרָה, הָיוּ כּוֹרְעִים וּמִשְׁתַּחֲוִים וְנוֹפְלִים עַל פְּנֵיהֶם, וְאוֹמְרִים: בָּרוּךְ שֵׁם כְּבוֹד מַלְכוּתוֹ לְעוֹלָם וָעֶד.

And the Kohanim and the nation of Israel who were standing in the Courtyard, when they heard the holy Name of Hashem coming so holy and pure from the mouth of the Kohen Gadol, they would kneel down onto the floor, give thanks, press their faces to the ground, and say, "Blessed is the Name of His wonderful Kingdom, forever and ever."

וְכַךְ הָיָה אוֹמֵר: אָנָּא הַשֵּׁם, חָטָאתִי, עָוִיתִי, פָּשַׁעְתִּי לְפָנֶיךָ אֲנִי וּבֵיתִי וּבְנֵי אַהֲרֹן עַם קְדוֹשֶׁךָ. אָנָּא בַשֵּׁם, כַּפֶּר נָא לַחֲטָאִים וְלַעֲוֹנוֹת וְלַפְּשָׁעִים שֶׁחָטָאתִי וְשֶׁעָוִיתִי וְשֶׁפָּשַׁעְתִּי לְפָנֶיךָ אֲנִי וּבֵיתִי וּבְנֵי אַהֲרֹן עַם קְדוֹשֶׁךָ, כַּכָּתוּב בְּתוֹרַת מֹשֶׁה עַבְדֶּךָ, מִפִּי כְבוֹדֶךָ: כִּי בַיּוֹם הַזֶּה יְכַפֵּר עֲלֵיכֶם לְטַהֵר אֶתְכֶם, מִכֹּל חַטֹּאתֵיכֶם לִפְנֵי יהוה -

And he (the Kohen) would say, "Please Hashem, I, my family, and the Kohanim have sinned by accident and on purpose also. I beg You to forgive us. As it is written in the Torah, given straight from Your mouth to Moshe Your servant: 'Because on this day (Yom Kippur) he (the Kohen) will atone for you to cleanse you and make you pure from all your sins, in front of Hashem.'"

We continue with the paragraph וְהַכֹּהֲנִים וְהָעָם.

Now we describe how the Kohen Gadol counted out loud when he sprinkled the blood of the sacrifices. We also say this count out loud.

וְכַךְ הָיָה מוֹנֶה: אַחַת, אַחַת וְאַחַת, אַחַת וּשְׁתַּיִם, אַחַת וְשָׁלֹשׁ, אַחַת וְאַרְבַּע, אַחַת וְחָמֵשׁ, אַחַת וָשֵׁשׁ, אַחַת וָשֶׁבַע.

And he (the Kohen Gadol) would count as he sprinkled the blood of the special Yom Kippur sacrifice, once upward, and seven times downward: one, one and one, one and two, one and three, one and four, one and five, one and six, one and seven.

And he (the Kohen) would say, "Please Hashem, Your nation has sinned by accident and on purpose also. I beg You to forgive them. As it is written in the Torah, given straight from Your mouth to Moshe Your servant: 'Because on this day (Yom Kippur) he (the Kohen) will atone for you to cleanse you and make you pure from all your sins, in front of Hashem.

וְכָךְ הָיָה אוֹמֵר: אָנָּא הַשֵּׁם, חָטָאוּ, עָווּ, פָּשְׁעוּ לְפָנֶיךָ עַמְּךָ בֵּית יִשְׂרָאֵל. אָנָּא בַשֵּׁם, כַּפֶּר נָא לַחֲטָאִים וְלַעֲוֹנוֹת וְלַפְּשָׁעִים שֶׁחָטְאוּ,וְשֶׁעָווּ וְשֶׁפָּשְׁעוּ לְפָנֶיךָ עַמְּךָ בֵּית יִשְׂרָאֵל, כַּכָּתוּב בְּתוֹרַת מֹשֶׁה עַבְדֶּךָ, מִפִּי כְבוֹדֶךָ: כִּי בַיּוֹם הַזֶּה יְכַפֵּר עֲלֵיכֶם לְטַהֵר אֶתְכֶם, מִכֹּל חַטֹּאתֵיכֶם לִפְנֵי יהוה -

We continue with the paragraph וְהַכֹּהֲנִים וְהָעָם.

Did You Know??
We are not allowed to bow down on our knees on a floor outside the *Beis HaMikdash*. Therefore, when we bow on our knees during *Aleinu*, we make sure to put something (a towel or paper) under our knees so that we do not directly touch the floor.

Did You Know??
The purpose of the Temple Service performed on Yom Kippur by the Kohen Gadol was to bring forgiveness to the entire Jewish nation.

Our Sages teach that by saying and studying the service, it is like we actually did it.

A Closer Look
There were many details of the Temple Service that were commanded by Hashem for the Kohen Gadol to do on Yom Kippur.

A Closer Look
The Kohen Gadol would count out loud so as not to take even the smallest chance of making a mistake. He did not want to skip a sprinkling, or do any sprinkling even one extra time.

עֲשָׂרָה הֲרוּגֵי מַלְכוּת / *Asarah Harugei Malchus*

This is the opening verse of a *piyut*, a poetic prayer, that most congregations recite aloud, verse by verse.

אֵלֶּה אֶזְכְּרָה וְנַפְשִׁי עָלַי אֶשְׁפְּכָה,

I will remember these people (who died for the sake of the Name of Hashem), and I pour out my heart which is melting.

כִּי בְלָעוּנוּ זֵדִים כְּעֻגָּה בְּלִי הֲפוּכָה,

Strangers have destroyed me, like I was a thin piece of wafer.

כִּי בִימֵי הַשָּׂר לֹא עָלְתָה אֲרוּכָה, לַעֲשָׂרָה הֲרוּגֵי מְלוּכָה.

When the Roman ruler ruled, there was no relief for anyone, and surely not for the ten *tzaddikim* who were murdered by the government.

Did You Know??
The story of these Ten Martyrs is also told on Tishah B'Av.

A Closer Look

A Roman ruler asked the Rabbis to tell him what the Torah says about a person who kidnaps another Jew and then sells him. They explained that such a person is put to death. Hadrian told them that *they* should be put to death, since they are the descendants of the ten sons of Yaakov, who kidnapped their younger brother Yosef and sold him. (He was then brought down to Egypt.) Some Rabbis teach us that these ten Sages were murdered as an atonement for the Jewish people because of this sin committed by the ten sons of Yaakov.

But to the ruler, this was all just an excuse. In fact, he wanted the Rabbis killed because they were teaching Torah to the Jewish People.

Did You Know??

This prayer was composed by an unknown poet whose name was Yehudah. Its verses begin with the letter *aleph*, and end with the letter *taf*.

The Ten Martyrs include:

Rabbi Akiva — He began to learn Torah at the age of 40. He became the greatest Torah scholar of his generation. He taught tens of thousands of students. For teaching Torah, the Romans killed him. They ripped the flesh off his body with sharp combs. While being killed, he recited the *Shema*, thanking Hashem for letting him die for His sake. He finally died while reciting the word "*Echad* — One."

Rabbi Yehudah ben Damah — Little is known of him besides the fact that he was one of the Ten Martyrs.

Rabbi Chananya ben Teradyon — The Romans brought him from the *beis midrash* and wrapped his body in a Torah Scroll. They also covered his body with water-soaked wool, so that when they burnt him to death, the pain would last longer. The letters of the Torah flew up to Heaven as the Torah was being burnt together with him. The Roman guard asked is he would receive a share in the World to Come if he removed the wool. Rabbi Chananya said yes. The soldier removed the wool and jumped into the flames.

Rabbi Yehudah ben Bava — He openly defied the Roman law that forbade teaching Torah. He gave *semichah* to five of Rabbi Akiva's best students. When the Romans caught him doing this, he told the students to run, but he was too old to escape. He remained there. The Romans shot him with arrows over and over till he died.

Rabbi Chutzpis Meturgeman (the interpreter) — He was called this because he would explain the words of the head of the yeshivah to the masses so that everyone would understand what was being taught.

Rabbi Yeshevav Sofer (the Scribe) — He was a colleague of Rabbi Akiva.

Rabbi Elazar ben Shamua — He was one of the five best students of Rabbi Akiva.

Rabbi Chaninah ben Chachinai — He was one of the first students of Rabbi Akiva.

Rabbi Shimon ben Gamliel — He was the *Nasi*, the Prince of the Jewish People. He begged the Romans to kill him before Rabbi Yishmael so that he would not have to witness him being killed.

Rabbi Yishmael — He was the Kohen Gadol. The angel Gabriel explained to him that he and the other rabbis would be killed to sanctify Hashem's Name.

A Closer Look

These are the stories of the Ten Martyrs, leaders of the Jewish people who were murdered by the Romans. They lived during the 130-year period when the Mishnah was written — from the years 70 until 200. At that time, the Romans ruled over the Land of Israel.

These ten *tzaddikim* were not all murdered at the same time, but our tradition links them together to show how cruel the Romans were to our people.

מַפְטִיר יוֹנָה / *Sefer Yonah*

At *Minchah* on Yom Kippur, we read the Book of *Yonah*, one of the Twelve Prophets (*Trei Asar*), as the *Haftarah*.

The English beneath the Hebrew text is a concise adaptation of the story.

א וַיְהִי דְּבַר־יהוה אֶל־יוֹנָה בֶן־אֲמִתַּי
לֵאמֹר: ב קוּם לֵךְ אֶל־נִינְוֵה הָעִיר הַגְּדוֹלָה
וּקְרָא עָלֶיהָ כִּי־עָלְתָה רָעָתָם לְפָנָי: ג וַיָּקָם
יוֹנָה לִבְרֹחַ תַּרְשִׁישָׁה מִלִּפְנֵי יהוה וַיֵּרֶד יָפוֹ
וַיִּמְצָא אֳנִיָּה | בָּאָה תַרְשִׁישׁ וַיִּתֵּן שְׂכָרָהּ וַיֵּרֶד
בָּהּ לָבוֹא עִמָּהֶם תַּרְשִׁישָׁה מִלִּפְנֵי יהוה:
ד וַיהוה הֵטִיל רוּחַ־גְּדוֹלָה אֶל־הַיָּם וַיְהִי סַעַר־
גָּדוֹל בַּיָּם וְהָאֳנִיָּה חִשְּׁבָה לְהִשָּׁבֵר: ה וַיִּירְאוּ
הַמַּלָּחִים וַיִּזְעֲקוּ אִישׁ אֶל־אֱלֹהָיו וַיָּטִלוּ אֶת־
הַכֵּלִים אֲשֶׁר בָּאֳנִיָּה אֶל־הַיָּם לְהָקֵל מֵעֲלֵיהֶם
וְיוֹנָה יָרַד אֶל־יַרְכְּתֵי הַסְּפִינָה וַיִּשְׁכַּב וַיֵּרָדַם:
ו וַיִּקְרַב אֵלָיו רַב הַחֹבֵל וַיֹּאמֶר לוֹ מַה־לְּךָ
נִרְדָּם קוּם קְרָא אֶל־אֱלֹהֶיךָ אוּלַי יִתְעַשֵּׁת
הָאֱלֹהִים לָנוּ וְלֹא נֹאבֵד: ז וַיֹּאמְרוּ אִישׁ אֶל־
רֵעֵהוּ לְכוּ וְנַפִּילָה גוֹרָלוֹת וְנֵדְעָה בְּשֶׁלְּמִי
הָרָעָה הַזֹּאת לָנוּ וַיַּפִּלוּ גּוֹרָלוֹת וַיִּפֹּל הַגּוֹרָל
עַל־יוֹנָה: ח וַיֹּאמְרוּ אֵלָיו הַגִּידָה־נָּא לָנוּ בַּאֲשֶׁר
לְמִי־הָרָעָה הַזֹּאת לָנוּ מַה־מְּלַאכְתְּךָ וּמֵאַיִן

תָּבוֹא מָה אַרְצֶךָ וְאֵי־מִזֶּה עַם אָתָּה: ט וַיֹּאמֶר
אֲלֵיהֶם עִבְרִי אָנֹכִי וְאֶת־יהוה אֱלֹהֵי הַשָּׁמַיִם
אֲנִי יָרֵא אֲשֶׁר־עָשָׂה אֶת־הַיָּם וְאֶת־הַיַּבָּשָׁה:
י וַיִּירְאוּ הָאֲנָשִׁים יִרְאָה גְדוֹלָה וַיֹּאמְרוּ אֵלָיו
מַה־זֹּאת עָשִׂיתָ כִּי־יָדְעוּ הָאֲנָשִׁים כִּי־מִלִּפְנֵי
יהוה הוּא בֹרֵחַ כִּי הִגִּיד לָהֶם: יא וַיֹּאמְרוּ אֵלָיו
מַה־נַּעֲשֶׂה לָּךְ וְיִשְׁתֹּק הַיָּם מֵעָלֵינוּ כִּי הַיָּם
הוֹלֵךְ וְסֹעֵר: יב וַיֹּאמֶר אֲלֵיהֶם שָׂאוּנִי וַהֲטִילֻנִי
אֶל־הַיָּם וְיִשְׁתֹּק הַיָּם מֵעֲלֵיכֶם כִּי יוֹדֵעַ אָנִי כִּי
בְשֶׁלִּי הַסַּעַר הַגָּדוֹל הַזֶּה עֲלֵיכֶם: יג וַיַּחְתְּרוּ
הָאֲנָשִׁים לְהָשִׁיב אֶל־הַיַּבָּשָׁה וְלֹא יָכֹלוּ כִּי
הַיָּם הוֹלֵךְ וְסֹעֵר עֲלֵיהֶם: יד וַיִּקְרְאוּ אֶל־יהוה
וַיֹּאמְרוּ אָנָּה יהוה אַל־נָא נֹאבְדָה בְּנֶפֶשׁ
הָאִישׁ הַזֶּה וְאַל־תִּתֵּן עָלֵינוּ דָּם
נָקִיא כִּי־אַתָּה יהוה
כַּאֲשֶׁר חָפַצְתָּ

עֲשִׂיתָ: טו וַיִּשְׂאוּ אֶת־יוֹנָה וַיְטִלֻהוּ אֶל־הַיָּם וַיַּעֲמֹד הַיָּם מִזַּעְפּוֹ: טז וַיִּירְאוּ הָאֲנָשִׁים יִרְאָה גְדוֹלָה אֶת־יְהוָה וַיִּזְבְּחוּ־זֶבַח לַיהוָה וַיִּדְּרוּ נְדָרִים: ב א וַיְמַן יְהוָה דָּג גָּדוֹל לִבְלֹעַ אֶת־יוֹנָה וַיְהִי יוֹנָה בִּמְעֵי הַדָּג שְׁלֹשָׁה יָמִים וּשְׁלֹשָׁה לֵילוֹת: ב וַיִּתְפַּלֵּל יוֹנָה אֶל־יְהוָה אֱלֹהָיו מִמְּעֵי הַדָּגָה: ג וַיֹּאמֶר קָרָאתִי מִצָּרָה לִי אֶל־יְהוָה וַיַּעֲנֵנִי מִבֶּטֶן שְׁאוֹל שִׁוַּעְתִּי שָׁמַעְתָּ קוֹלִי: ד וַתַּשְׁלִיכֵנִי מְצוּלָה בִּלְבַב יַמִּים וְנָהָר יְסֹבְבֵנִי כָּל־מִשְׁבָּרֶיךָ וְגַלֶּיךָ עָלַי עָבָרוּ: ה וַאֲנִי אָמַרְתִּי נִגְרַשְׁתִּי מִנֶּגֶד עֵינֶיךָ אַךְ אוֹסִיף לְהַבִּיט אֶל־הֵיכַל קָדְשֶׁךָ: ו אֲפָפוּנִי מַיִם עַד־נֶפֶשׁ תְּהוֹם יְסֹבְבֵנִי סוּף חָבוּשׁ לְרֹאשִׁי: ז לְקִצְבֵי הָרִים יָרַדְתִּי הָאָרֶץ בְּרִחֶיהָ בַעֲדִי לְעוֹלָם וַתַּעַל מִשַּׁחַת חַיַּי יְהוָה אֱלֹהָי: ח בְּהִתְעַטֵּף עָלַי נַפְשִׁי אֶת־יְהוָה זָכָרְתִּי וַתָּבוֹא אֵלֶיךָ תְּפִלָּתִי אֶל־הֵיכַל קָדְשֶׁךָ: ט מְשַׁמְּרִים הַבְלֵי־שָׁוְא חַסְדָּם

יַעֲזֹבוּ: י וַאֲנִי בְּקוֹל תּוֹדָה אֶזְבְּחָה־לָּךְ אֲשֶׁר נָדַרְתִּי אֲשַׁלֵּמָה יְשׁוּעָתָה לַיהוָה: יא וַיֹּאמֶר יְהוָה לַדָּג וַיָּקֵא אֶת־יוֹנָה אֶל־הַיַּבָּשָׁה: ג א וַיְהִי דְבַר־יְהוָה אֶל־יוֹנָה שֵׁנִית לֵאמֹר: ב קוּם לֵךְ אֶל־נִינְוֵה הָעִיר הַגְּדוֹלָה וּקְרָא אֵלֶיהָ אֶת־הַקְּרִיאָה אֲשֶׁר אָנֹכִי דֹּבֵר אֵלֶיךָ: ג וַיָּקָם יוֹנָה וַיֵּלֶךְ אֶל־נִינְוֵה כִּדְבַר יְהוָה וְנִינְוֵה הָיְתָה עִיר־גְּדוֹלָה לֵאלֹהִים מַהֲלַךְ שְׁלֹשֶׁת יָמִים: ד וַיָּחֶל יוֹנָה לָבוֹא בָעִיר מַהֲלַךְ יוֹם אֶחָד וַיִּקְרָא וַיֹּאמַר עוֹד אַרְבָּעִים יוֹם וְנִינְוֵה נֶהְפָּכֶת: ה וַיַּאֲמִינוּ אַנְשֵׁי נִינְוֵה בֵּאלֹהִים וַיִּקְרְאוּ־צוֹם וַיִּלְבְּשׁוּ שַׂקִּים מִגְּדוֹלָם וְעַד־קְטַנָּם: ו וַיִּגַּע הַדָּבָר אֶל־מֶלֶךְ נִינְוֵה וַיָּקָם מִכִּסְאוֹ וַיַּעֲבֵר אַדַּרְתּוֹ מֵעָלָיו וַיְכַס שַׂק וַיֵּשֶׁב עַל־הָאֵפֶר: ז וַיַּזְעֵק וַיֹּאמֶר בְּנִינְוֵה מִטַּעַם הַמֶּלֶךְ וּגְדֹלָיו לֵאמֹר הָאָדָם וְהַבְּהֵמָה הַבָּקָר וְהַצֹּאן אַל־יִטְעֲמוּ מְאוּמָה אַל־יִרְעוּ וּמַיִם אַל־יִשְׁתּוּ: ח וְיִתְכַּסּוּ שַׂקִּים

"Go to Nineveh," Hashem commanded Yonah. "The people there are very wicked. Tell them they will be destroyed."

Yonah did not want to go to speak to the people of Nineveh. He decided instead to run away to Tarshish on a boat.

While the boat was at sea, a strong wind began blowing. It turned into a mighty storm. The ship was tossed up and down. It looked like the ship would break apart. The sailors became frightened. "Everyone pray so that we may be saved!" they shouted. Then they began to throw objects into the ocean to make the boat lighter.

"The storm is not stopping!" the people yelled. "Maybe there is a wicked man on the ship and we are being punished because of him. Let us cast lots and see whose fault it is." The lot fell upon Yonah.

"This storm is indeed because of me," Yonah said. "I am trying to run away from doing what Hashem commanded. That is why this is happening. Throw me into the sea and you will see that the storm will calm down."

They did not want to throw Yonah overboard. They tried to return to land instead, but the storm continued in its full strength.

הָאָדָ֗ם וְהַבְּהֵמָ֔ה וְיִקְרְא֥וּ אֶל־אֱלֹהִ֖ים בְּחׇזְקָ֑ה וְיָשֻׁ֗בוּ אִ֚ישׁ מִדַּרְכּ֣וֹ הָֽרָעָ֔ה וּמִן־הֶחָמָ֖ס אֲשֶׁ֥ר בְּכַפֵּיהֶֽם׃ ט מִֽי־יוֹדֵ֣עַ יָשׁ֔וּב וְנִחַ֖ם הָאֱלֹהִ֑ים וְשָׁ֛ב מֵחֲר֥וֹן אַפּ֖וֹ וְלֹ֥א נֹאבֵֽד׃ י וַיַּ֤רְא הָֽאֱלֹהִים֙ אֶֽת־מַ֣עֲשֵׂיהֶ֔ם כִּי־שָׁ֖בוּ מִדַּרְכָּ֣ם הָרָעָ֑ה וַיִּנָּ֣חֶם הָאֱלֹהִ֗ים עַל־הָרָעָ֛ה אֲשֶׁר־דִּבֶּ֥ר לַעֲשׂוֹת־לָהֶ֖ם וְלֹ֥א עָשָֽׂה׃ ד א וַיֵּ֥רַע אֶל־יוֹנָ֖ה רָעָ֣ה גְדוֹלָ֑ה וַיִּ֖חַר לֽוֹ׃ ב וַיִּתְפַּלֵּ֣ל אֶל־יְהֹוָ֗ה וַיֹּאמַ֡ר אָנָּ֣ה יְהֹוָה֩ הֲלוֹא־זֶ֨ה דְבָרִ֜י עַד־הֱיוֹתִ֣י עַל־אַדְמָתִ֗י עַל־כֵּ֤ן קִדַּ֙מְתִּי֙ לִבְרֹ֣חַ תַּרְשִׁ֔ישָׁה כִּ֣י יָדַ֗עְתִּי כִּ֣י אַתָּ֞ה אֵֽל־חַנּ֤וּן וְרַחוּם֙ אֶ֣רֶךְ אַפַּ֔יִם וְרַב־חֶ֔סֶד וְנִחָ֖ם עַל־הָרָעָֽה׃ ג וְעַתָּ֣ה יְהֹוָ֔ה קַח־נָ֥א אֶת־נַפְשִׁ֖י מִמֶּ֑נִּי כִּ֛י ט֥וֹב מוֹתִ֖י מֵחַיָּֽי׃ ד וַיֹּ֣אמֶר יְהֹוָ֔ה הַהֵיטֵ֖ב חָ֥רָה לָֽךְ׃ ה וַיֵּצֵ֤א יוֹנָה֙ מִן־הָעִ֔יר וַיֵּ֖שֶׁב מִקֶּ֣דֶם לָעִ֑יר וַיַּ֩עַשׂ֩ ל֨וֹ שָׁ֜ם סֻכָּ֗ה וַיֵּ֤שֶׁב תַּחְתֶּ֙יהָ֙ בַּצֵּ֔ל עַ֚ד אֲשֶׁ֣ר יִרְאֶ֔ה מַה־יִּהְיֶ֖ה בָּעִֽיר׃ ו וַיְמַ֣ן יְהֹוָֽה־אֱ֠לֹהִ֠ים קִיקָי֞וֹן וַיַּ֣עַל ׀ מֵעַ֣ל לְיוֹנָ֗ה לִהְי֥וֹת צֵל֙ עַל־רֹאשׁ֔וֹ

לְהַצִּ֥יל ל֖וֹ מֵרָעָת֑וֹ וַיִּשְׂמַ֤ח יוֹנָה֙ עַל־הַקִּ֣יקָי֔וֹן שִׂמְחָ֥ה גְדוֹלָֽה׃ ז וַיְמַ֤ן הָֽאֱלֹהִים֙ תּוֹלַ֔עַת בַּעֲל֥וֹת הַשַּׁ֖חַר לַמׇּחֳרָ֑ת וַתַּ֥ךְ אֶת־הַקִּֽיקָי֖וֹן וַיִּיבָֽשׁ׃ ח וַיְהִ֣י ׀ כִּזְרֹ֣חַ הַשֶּׁ֗מֶשׁ וַיְמַ֨ן אֱלֹהִ֜ים ר֤וּחַ קָדִים֙ חֲרִישִׁ֔ית וַתַּ֥ךְ הַשֶּׁ֛מֶשׁ עַל־רֹ֥אשׁ יוֹנָ֖ה וַיִּתְעַלָּ֑ף וַיִּשְׁאַ֤ל אֶת־נַפְשׁוֹ֙ לָמ֔וּת וַיֹּ֕אמֶר ט֥וֹב מוֹתִ֖י מֵחַיָּֽי׃ ט וַיֹּ֤אמֶר אֱלֹהִים֙ אֶל־יוֹנָ֔ה הַהֵיטֵ֥ב חָרָֽה־לְךָ֖ עַל־הַקִּֽיקָי֑וֹן וַיֹּ֕אמֶר הֵיטֵ֥ב חָֽרָה־לִ֖י עַד־מָֽוֶת׃ י וַיֹּ֣אמֶר יְהֹוָ֔ה אַתָּ֥ה חַ֙סְתָּ֙ עַל־הַקִּ֣יקָי֔וֹן אֲשֶׁ֛ר לֹא־עָמַ֥לְתָּ בּ֖וֹ וְלֹ֣א גִדַּלְתּ֑וֹ שֶׁבִּן־לַ֥יְלָה הָיָ֖ה וּבִן־לַ֥יְלָה אָבָֽד׃ יא וַֽאֲנִי֙ לֹ֣א אָח֔וּס עַל־נִֽינְוֵ֖ה הָעִ֣יר הַגְּדוֹלָ֑ה אֲשֶׁ֣ר יֶשׁ־בָּ֡הּ הַרְבֵּה֩ מִֽשְׁתֵּים־עֶשְׂרֵ֨ה רִבּ֜וֹ אָדָ֗ם אֲשֶׁ֤ר לֹֽא־יָדַע֙ בֵּין־יְמִינ֣וֹ לִשְׂמֹאל֔וֹ וּבְהֵמָ֖ה רַבָּֽה׃

מיכה יח-כ

יח מִי־אֵ֣ל כָּמ֗וֹךָ נֹשֵׂ֤א עָוֺן֙ וְעֹבֵ֣ר עַל־פֶּ֔שַׁע לִשְׁאֵרִ֖ית נַחֲלָת֑וֹ לֹא־הֶחֱזִ֤יק לָעַד֙ אַפּ֔וֹ כִּֽי־חָפֵ֥ץ חֶ֖סֶד הֽוּא׃ יט יָשׁ֣וּב יְרַחֲמֵ֔נוּ יִכְבֹּ֖שׁ עֲוֺנֹתֵ֑ינוּ וְתַשְׁלִ֛יךְ בִּמְצֻל֥וֹת יָ֖ם כׇּל־חַטֹּאותָֽם׃ כ תִּתֵּ֤ן אֱמֶת֙ לְיַֽעֲקֹ֔ב חֶ֖סֶד לְאַבְרָהָ֑ם אֲשֶׁר־נִשְׁבַּ֥עְתָּ לַאֲבֹתֵ֖ינוּ מִ֥ימֵי קֶֽדֶם׃

They threw Yonah into the sea and the storm stopped. Then, a giant fish came and swallowed Yonah.

For three days and three nights, Yonah was in the belly of the fish. He prayed to Hashem, "Please save me, and I will bring sacrifices to You." Hashem heard his prayers and the fish spat Yonah out onto the dry land.

Again Hashem commanded Yonah, "Go to Nineveh and tell them my message." This time Yonah listened and went to Nineveh.

Yonah stood in the middle of the city and said, "In forty days Nineveh will be destroyed."

The people believed in Hashem. The whole city fasted. They repented and stopped doing evil. They returned all the stolen property they had taken.

Hashem saw that they repented and forgave them. They were not punished.

After this, Yonah felt sad that they had repented and his prophecy was not fulfilled. Yonah went into the desert. It was very hot and dry. Hashem wanted to teach Yonah a lesson. Hashem created a *kikayon* (a kind of shady plant) to shade him from the sun. *I am so thankful to Hashem for giving me this shade*, Yonah thought.

The next day Hashem created a worm that destroyed the *kikayon*. Yonah was very sad.

Hashem said to Yonah. "You are sad because one *kikayon* tree was destroyed. Shouldn't I take pity upon a whole city, which would have been wiped out if they did not repent?"

Did You Know??
Hashem created the *kikayon* to teach Yonah a lesson. Hashem has pity on all His creations. All they need to do is truly repent.

A Closer Look
We read this *Haftarah* on Yom Kippur because it shows just how powerful repentance is. Even though the people of Nineveh sinned, once they honestly repented, Hashem forgave them, and did not punish them. Moreover, the people of Nineveh were idol worshipers. If Hashem will forgive idol worshipers who repent, surely He will forgive His people, the Jewish nation, if they repent.

A Closer Look
Why didn't Yonah want to go to Nineveh? How could he not go after Hashem commanded him to go? It is because Yonah was afraid that the people of Nineveh would repent and the Jewish people would not. Then the Jewish people would be severely punished.

נְעִילָה / Ne'ilah

Yom Kippur is the high point of the Ten Days of Repentance that start with Rosh Hashanah. *Ne'ilah*, the time of the "closing of the gates" is the "high" point of Yom Kippur. This is the holiest time of the year, and our last chance to have our prayers accepted by Hashem on Yom Kippur, the day especially given to us for *teshuvah*.

In *Shemoneh Esrei*, we change some of the phrases we added from Rosh Hashanah to Yom Kippur, because the Book of Life is now being sealed.

Remember us for life, Hashem, Who wants life. And seal us in the Book of Life — for Your sake.

זָכְרֵנוּ לְחַיִּים, מֶלֶךְ חָפֵץ בַּחַיִּים, וְחָתְמֵנוּ בְּסֵפֶר הַחַיִּים, לְמַעַנְךָ אֱלֹהִים חַיִּים.

And seal all Jews, the children of Your covenant, for a good life.

וַחֲתוֹם לְחַיִּים טוֹבִים כָּל בְּנֵי בְרִיתֶךָ.

In the book of life, blessing, peace, and livelihood, may You remember us and seal us and Your whole nation, the Jewish people, for a good and peaceful life.

בְּסֵפֶר חַיִּים בְּרָכָה וְשָׁלוֹם, וּפַרְנָסָה טוֹבָה, נִזָּכֵר וְנֵחָתֵם לְפָנֶיךָ, אֲנַחְנוּ וְכָל עַמְּךָ בֵּית יִשְׂרָאֵל, לְחַיִּים טוֹבִים וּלְשָׁלוֹם.

Did You Know??
Wherever in the *Shemoneh Esrei* we asked Hashem to "write us" for a good and healthy life, we now say "seal us" instead; because now the Book of Life is being sealed.

The same is true when we say *Avinu Malkeinu*. Wherever we said "write us ...", we now say "seal us ..." instead.

A Closer Look
During Rosh Hashanah and Yom Kippur, everyone's fate is written in the Book of Life. It is during *Ne'ilah* that everyone's fate is sealed.

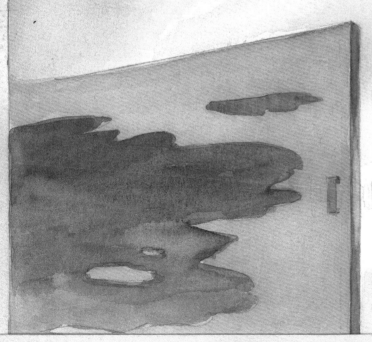
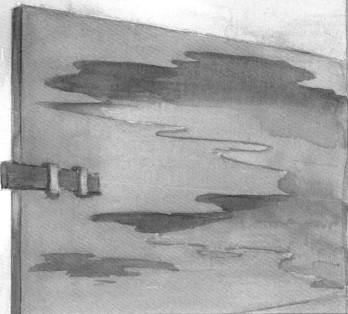

סְלִיחוֹת / *Selichos*

We say *Selichos* during *Ne'ilah*. This prayer is the special formula Hashem taught Moshe for the Jewish people to use to beg forgiveness.

וַיַּעֲבֹר יהוה עַל פָּנָיו וַיִּקְרָא:

And Hashem passed before him (Moshe)
and He called out (teaching Moshe this special prayer):

יהוה, יהוה, אֵל, רַחוּם, וְחַנּוּן, אֶרֶךְ אַפַּיִם, וְרַב חֶסֶד, וֶאֱמֶת, נֹצֵר חֶסֶד לָאֲלָפִים, נֹשֵׂא עָוֹן, וָפֶשַׁע, וְחַטָּאָה, וְנַקֵּה.

Hashem, Hashem, God, Merciful and Gracious, Slow to anger,
and Full of Kindness and Truth, Who Records Kindness for thousands of generations,
Who is the Forgiver of sin, and mistakes, and Who cleanses.

A Closer Look

After leaving Egypt, *Bnei Yisrael* sinned in the desert. They thought Moshe was late in returning from Har Sinai and that he probably had died. The people felt they had no one to turn to, and they were afraid. They created and worshiped a Golden Calf. Hashem was very angry at them for this sin. Moshe prayed to Hashem to forgive His people. Hashem then told Moshe, "I will teach you a special prayer. Whenever I am angry at the Jewish People, they can say this and I will forgive them."

Did You Know??

The word "*Selichos*" means forgiveness.

A Closer Look

As Yom Kippur ends, we say this prayer knowing that even if we had to give up our lives for Hashem, we would.

The *chazzan* first says and then the entire congregation says together and out loud:

שְׁמַע יִשְׂרָאֵל, יהוה אֱלֹהֵינוּ, יהוה אֶחָד.

Hear, O Israel, Hashem is our God, Hashem is the only One.

The *chazzan* first says three times, and then the entire congregation says three times, together and out loud:

בָּרוּךְ שֵׁם כְּבוֹד מַלְכוּתוֹ לְעוֹלָם וָעֶד.

Blessed is the Name of His wonderful kingdom forever and ever.

A Closer Look

Yom Kippur is about to end. This means that we are about to fall from the level of angels back to the level of normal people. We say this blessing of the angels one more time out loud, with all our might and concentration.

Did You Know??

This is said three times because Hashem was King before this world was created, Hashem is King over this world, and Hashem will be King over the World to Come.

A Closer Look

On Har Carmel, Eliyahu HaNavi proved that the prophets of King Achav were false prophets. Then, all the Children of Israel called out these words, "Hashem — only He is God." It became clear to everyone that the gods of stone and wood had no power at all; only Hashem was all-powerful.

Did You Know??

This is recited seven times because there are seven levels of Heaven. As Yom Kippur ends, we are, so to speak, escorting Hashem — Who "came down" to hear our prayers — back through the seven Heavens.

The *chazzan* first says seven times, then the entire congregation says seven times, together and out loud:

יהוה הוּא הָאֱלֹהִים.

Hashem — only He is God!

Kaddish is said and the final blast of the shofar is sounded.

Then the congregation says out loud and together:

לְשָׁנָה הַבָּאָה בִּירוּשָׁלָיִם.

Next year in Yerushalayim!

Did You Know??

Why is the shofar blown at the end of Yom Kippur? One reason is that Hashem's Presence was with us on Yom Kippur. At Har Sinai, the shofar blew when His Presence left. Now, too, as His Presence leaves, we blow the shofar.

And we hope that this shofar blast will bring closer the blowing of the "Great Shofar," the shofar that announces the coming of *Mashiach*.